TESTIMONIES

The Works of Patrick O'Brian

Biography

PICASSO
JOSEPH BANKS

Aubrey/Maturin Novels
in order of publication

MASTER AND COMMANDER
POST CAPTAIN
H.M.S. SURPRISE
THE MAURITIUS COMMAND
DESOLATION ISLAND
THE FORTUNE OF WAR
THE SURGEON'S MATE
THE IONIAN MISSION
TREASON'S HARBOUR
THE FAR SIDE OF THE WORLD
THE REVERSE OF THE MEDAL
THE LETTER OF MARQUE
THE THIRTEEN-GUN SALUTE
THE NUTMEG OF CONSOLATION
THE TRUELOVE
THE WINE-DARK SEA
THE COMMODORE
THE YELLOW ADMIRAL
THE HUNDRED DAYS
BLUE AT THE MIZZEN

Novels

TESTIMONIES
THE GOLDEN OCEAN
THE UNKNOWN SHORE

Collections

THE RENDEZVOUS AND OTHER STORIES

TESTIMONIES

Patrick O'Brian

W.W. NORTON & COMPANY
NEW YORK / LONDON

Printed in the United States of America

The text of this book is composed in 11/15 New Baskerville,
with the display set in Bernhard Modern Roman.
Composition and manufacturing by the Haddon Craftsmen, Inc.
Book design by Jo Anne Metsch.

Library of Congress Cataloging-in-Publication Data

O'Brian Patrick, 1914–
Testimonies / Patrick O'Brian.
p.   cm.
I. Title.
PR6029.B55T47   1993
823'.914—dc20   92-27426

ISBN 0-393-31316-6

W. W. Norton & Company, Inc.
500 Fifth Avenue, New York, N.Y. 10110
www.wwnorton.com

W. W. Norton & Company Ltd.
Castle House, 75/76 Wells Street, London W1T 3QT

For Mary, with love

Preface

T o read a first novel by an unknown author which, sentence by sentence and page by page, makes one say: he can't keep going at this pitch, the intensity is bound to break down, the perfection of tone can't be sustained—is to rejoice in an experience of pleasure and astonishment. Patrick O'Brian's *Testimonies* makes one think of a great ballad or a Biblical story. At first one thinks the book's emotional power is chiefly a triumph of style; and indeed the book is remarkable enough for the beauty and exactness of phrasing and rhythm which can only be characterized by quotation:

It was September when I first came into the valley: the top of it was hidden in fine rain, and the enclosing ridges on either side merged into a gray, formless cloud. There was no hint of the two peaks that were shown on the map, high and steep on each side of the valley's head. This I saw from the windows of the station cab as it brought me up the mountainous road from the plains, a road so narrow that in places the car could barely run between the stone walls. All the way I had been leaning forward in my seat, excited and eager to be impressed: at another time the precipices that appeared so frequently on the left hand would have made me uneasy, but now they were proofs of a strange and wilder land, and I was exhilarated.

. . . There may be things more absurd than a middle-aged man in the grip of a high-flung romantic passion: a boy can behave more foolishly, but at least in him it is natural.

I kept away. I read Burton in the mountains. We had a spell of idyllic weather, and the soft loving wind was a torment to me.

I would not pass those days again. I knew I was a ludicrous figure, and it hurt all the more. I did not eat. I could not read, I could not sleep. I walked and walked, and when one day I broke a tooth on a fruit stone I welcomed the pain.

Long before I had engaged to help with the yearly gathering of the sheep for the shearing, and now the time came around. The boy came up to ask if I would meet Emyr on the quarry road early the next morning. I wondered how I should face him, but there was nothing for it and I said I should be very glad.

But the reader soon forgets the style as such—a forgetting that is the greatest accomplishment of prose—in the enchantment and vividness of the story. John Aubrey Pugh, an Oxford don who has given up his teaching post and come to live in a secluded Welsh valley, falls in love wth Bronwen Vaughn, the wife of a young farmer who is his neighbor. She in turn, but less quickly, falls in love with him; and she is estranged from her husband, an admirable man in many ways, but one who has compelled her to submit to some unnamed, brutal sexual perversion. When a famous preacher whose advances she has rejected with contempt persuades the entire community that she has committed adultery with Pugh—an accusation which is false in a physical sense but true emotionally—she is poisoned or poisons herself. This summary is more unjust than most, for the comparative simplicity of the action when thus formulated conceals the labyrinthine complexity of attitude, motive, and feeling.

For example, Mr. Pugh and Mrs. Vaughn, as they call each other to the end, come to a recognition of their love for each other without speaking explicitly of love at all, while they are arguing mildly and pensively about whether civilization makes human beings happy or unhappy. The over-civilized man condemns civilization and the beautiful, spontaneous woman defends it, both of them unknowingly and passionately evaluating civilization as they do because they are in love with each other, the man condemning civilization because it is the great obstacle between him and another man's wife, the woman praising it because the man is entirely a product of it. The reader, drawn forward by lyric eloquence and the story's fascination, discovers in the end that he has encountered in a new way the sphinx and riddle of existence itself. What O'Brian has accomplished is literally and exactly the equivalent of some of the lyrics in Yeats' *The Tower* and *The Winding Stair* where within the colloquial and formal framework of the folk poem or story the greatest sophistication, consciousness and meaning become articulate. In

Preface

O'Brian, as in Yeats, the most studied literary cultivation and knowledge bring into being works which read as if they were prior to literature and conscious literary technique.

—Delmore Schwartz, in the *Partisan Review*, August 1952

TESTIMONIES

Pugh
===

"**M**r. Pugh, I came to ask you some questions about your life in Cwm Bugail and about Mrs. Vaughan of Gelli, Bronwen Vaughan. But now I think it would be better if you were to let me have a written account."

Pugh had been expecting this: he had been prepared for it ever since he had come to that place, but still it was a blow on his heart, and he could scarcely reply. He said, Yes, he would do his best.

"I am sure it would be less painful than being questioned, and it would be better from my point of view, I think. What I should like is a roughly chronological narrative, as full and discursive as possible—nothing elaborate, of course; nothing in the way of a formal, scholarly exposition: it is for my eye alone. You need not be afraid of being irrelevant; there is hardly anything you can write on this subject that will not be useful to me. There is no hurry, so do not press yourself;

but please remember that it should be comprehensive. I will come in from time to time to see how you are getting on."

When he had gone, Pugh sat down again. He wondered why he was so moved; he had hardened himself for this—he had even prepared some of his answers in advance. The things they wanted to know about had been continually in his mind or on the edge of it; but now it was as if the idea were new, and the memories broken open for the first time.

He began. At the top of the clean page he wrote *The Testimony of Joseph Aubrey Pugh,* and underlined it twice. Then he paused; he leaned back in his chair and let his mind slip into a reverie: for a long, long silent wait he sat motionless.

He wrote—

It was September when I first came into the valley: the top of it was hidden in fine rain, and the enclosing ridges on either side merged into a gray, formless cloud. There was no hint of the two peaks that were shown on the map, high and steep on each side of the valley's head. This I saw from the windows of the station cab as it brought me up the mountainous road from the plains, a road so narrow that in places the car could barely run between the stone walls. All the way I had been leaning forward in my seat, excited and eager to be impressed: at another time the precipices that appeared so frequently on the left hand would have made me uneasy, but now they were proofs of a strange and wilder land, and I was exhilarated.

I did not expect my cottage when the car stopped; indeed, I thought that the driver had pulled up again to open a cattle-gate. We had been climbing steadily the whole length of the road and now as I got out of the car the cloud blew cold and damp in wisps on my face. The cottage stood on the mountain-side, square on a little dug-in plateau that almost undermined the road. It was the smallest habitation I had ever seen; a white front with a green door between two windows, and a gray roof the size of a sheet.

The driver, a bull of a man and silent, gave me a grunt for my money, recognized the tip with "Ta" in a more civil tone, and backed rapidly away in the thickening mist. I stared about for a minute and then with a curious flutter of anticipation I walked up the path and in at the green door. My things had arrived: they were standing in the doorway of the little room on the right of the door and I kicked over them before I found a match and the lamp.

The golden light spreading as the lamp warmed showed beams and a wooden ceiling a few inches above my head; the floor was made of huge slate flags, and the moisture stood on them in tiny drops that flattened to wet footprints as I walked. Still with the same odd excitement I took the lamp and explored my dwelling: I found a much better room on the left of the front door—two windows and a boarded floor, a comfortable chair and a Turkey rug by the stove. The house was built with stone walls of great thickness and this gave the windowsills a depth and a value in a small room that I would not have expected. The far window looked straight out over the valley: I leaned on the sill and peered out down the slope. The last gray light and a parting in the mist showed a huddle of buildings down there; I supposed them to be the farm, and while I stared a light appeared, traveled steadily along to a door and vanished; a faint ghostliness filled the windows of the building and then the mist blotted it out.

Up the ladder-like stairs—I had to hold the treads with

one hand while I went up—up the nine flat rungs of this staircase were two A-shaped lofts, made by the sloping sides of the roof and the top of the ceilings below. One had a bed and a window. A lean-to at the back, a coal-hole and a dreary little lavatory tacked on behind completed the house. It appeared to me incredible that so much could have been packed into that toy box of a house.

I had taken Hafod by letter, sight unseen. At that time any small furnished place was difficult to find, and as this one promised tranquillity, remoteness and a certain degree of comfort, I had taken it without spending much time in reflection.

A retreat of this kind had become quite necessary for me: for the last few years my health had been declining, and my work had grown increasingly arduous. It was not that my duties in the university took up so many days in the term, nor that my research carried me along at an exhausting pace; it was my tutoring that wore me down. The young men who came to me did not seem to do very well, and my responsibility for their lack of improvement worried me more and more. It had come to the pitch where I was spending more time over their essays than ever they had spent; and with indifferent health I found that this frustrating, ungrateful task had become an almost intolerable burden. Many people supposed, I believe, that I should throw up my fellowship, and although it was wretchedly paid there were plenty of unfortunate devils who would have been glad of it: but that I could not do. With no private means and a name unknown outside my college and the small circle of palaeographers who had read my articles, it was impossible.

By finding this refuge, I hoped to make so complete a break with my established habits and discontents that I should return to them and to the writing of my book *(The Bestiary before Isidore of Seville)* with enough zeal to carry me through the term and the next few chapters. My idea was to do nothing very much, to read books unrelated to my trade, and to walk in the mountains when I felt like it, and to lie long in bed.

The place had another attraction: it lay in the very heart of North Wales, and for many years I had wished to know something of the country and the people. My great-grandfather (from whom I have my name of Pugh) had come from Wales before he had established himself as a draper in Liverpool, and I believe there was quite a strong Welsh tradition in our family as late as my father's time. He, poor man, had been left a genteel competence by his draper grandfather; it had descended to him through his un-draper father, who had married a lady of very good family and dealt in large mercantile transactions, far from the counter. My father, a sociable man, living in a time of acute social distinctions, felt the Liverpool-Welsh side of his ancestry keenly. He dropped all Welsh contacts and added his mother's name, Aubrey, to ours. He had never cared for me to ask him about it, and he was not pleased when I took to studying the language—it was a fit of enthusiasm caused by my friendship with Annwyl, and it lasted several terms in my undergraduate days.

By the time I had sorted my belongings into some degree of order it was quite dark, and I was hungry. The lighting of the fire had taken me longer than I supposed it would, and now I was faced with a plunge down the wet, unknown mountain-side in the dark, for it was my intention to make acquaintance with the farm and to buy some eggs and milk for my supper.

The walk was quite as bad as I had foreseen; twice I scrambled over dry-stone walls, dislodging the top-most stones, and once there was a flurry of beasts—sheep, I imagined—as I came awkwardly over, and half-seen forms rushed wildly into the mist. After an indeterminate period of wandering, I found myself ankle-deep in a stream, with very little remaining idea of the relative position of my cottage or the farm. At this point a furious barking of dogs on my left served as a guide, and I followed the stream down to a path, from which I could see the lamp-lit windows of the farm.

I had some difficulty in finding the right door: the darkness was filled with angry dogs, whose clamor scattered my wits; but in time my knocking brought a staring gowk of a boy. He stood in the vague light of a glimmer that reached the passage from a lighted room behind; he fled at the sound of my voice, leaving me half in and half out, still exposed to the attack of the dogs. I had always been foolishly timid with animals; and these, conscious of their advantage, bullied me without mercy. A clash of boots in the farmyard, and a man's angry voice raised in Welsh oaths rescued me from this persecution; the dogs ceased, and the unseen figure addressed me, again in Welsh. In my agitation I could think of nothing better to say than, "I beg your pardon?"

"Oh; it is the gentleman from Hafod. Walk in, mister," he said; and as he spoke the far door opened and the light showed me the way to the kitchen. As I came in two old people stood up and turned expectant, even anxious faces toward me.

"It is the gentleman from Hafod," said the man behind me; but they were fluttered, and did not understand. He spoke again, quickly, in an undertone in Welsh, and their faces changed. The old lady hurried across the fireplace and placed the good chair by it, dislodging a cat and patting the cushion.

"Sit down, mister," she said, with a hesitant, unfinished gesture toward the chair, and the men said, "Sit down." She was very slight and frail; long ago she must have been beautiful; her faded blue eyes behind their steel-rimmed spectacles had the kindest expression and her face was set in the wrinkles that are caused by having worn a pleasant look for a lifetime. She stood with her hands folded and murmured, "Well, well," in a gentle, embarrassed tone.

It was an enormous room, and the far walls hardly threw back the light of the lamp on the table. I had a general impression of great length and breadth, beams, two dressers with rows of plates, a long white table in the middle, and an undulating slate floor; fire and brass at my left hand, and a high mantelpiece with a clock, and a gun hanging above it.

The old man was sitting on a dark, narrow bench that ran along the wall by the window: the youth I had seen first stood awkwardly by the angle of the far dresser, staring at me without a movement. There was an uncomfortable moment of silence before the old man said, "How you like Wales?" He spoke in a harsh, grating voice, with so strong an accent that the simple phrase was barely comprehensible. His three-toothed stubbly face was advanced with an expectant smile, so pleasant that I felt my own answering smile spread even before I had quite pieced together the words. I said that I liked it very much, and that this valley in particular delighted me. The old man did not understand more than the general drift: he said, "Oh?" in the deaf tone of incomprehension, and after a moment he said that he had been in the valley for forty-seven years.

"It is telling me she is seeing a light in Hafod," said the old lady. I told them that I had not expected to come until tomorrow (which they knew), that I had left my coming down to the farm later than I had meant, and that I had found it difficult to follow the right path. The three of them—for the younger man had finished with his boots and had come forward—listened with close attention, the strained attention of those listening to an unfamiliar voice talking a foreign language. Halfway through my recital I saw the folding intelligence die out of the eyes of the old people, but the younger man understood me very well. They were concerned that I had not been able to strike the path at once, and described the alternate ways.

"You must go by the *beudy* and then behind the *tŷ gwair:* you cannot miss it," said the young man, and the elders, with their faces turned toward him, nodded at the words. A blurting guffaw came from the youth by the dresser and cut the repeated direction short: finding himself observed and at a disadvantage, the youth fell silent as suddenly as he had burst out, and after a wretched moment squeezed himself out through the door.

The younger man pulled up a chair and sat by me. We talked about the cottage, postal deliveries, buses—the commonplaces of new arrival. He was a tall man, spare, red-haired with pale eyes and a thin, stretched skin: a reddish stubble on his chin, and papery, windbitten ears. His English was good, but he was nervous, and made mistakes. He listened attentively, leaning forward when I spoke, and answered my questions with anxious care: I felt that if a great land-owner of the Middle Ages had come into a farmhouse, this was the manner in which he would have been answered. I hoped that they had not some mistaken idea—did not suppose me to be a person of importance.

The others did not join in any more, though the old lady hovered by, looking at her son with a proud smile: I presumed he was her son, although there was no likeness between them. I was talking about the length of the journey (an unusually tedious train and several changes) when the door opened and a young woman came in, carrying a pile of clothes. I broke off, and the young man said, "Bronwen, here is the gentleman from Hafod."

She was obviously surprised and a little put about: her hand went up to her hair. But she put the clothes down on the dresser and came forward to meet me with none of the awkwardness that I should have shown in the same case. It was charming to see her come the length of the room: she was about thirty—not a girl—but she held herself with adolescent grace. She was extraordinarily good-looking. We shook hands, and she offered me a cup of tea; I refused, saying that I had just come down in the hope of being allowed to buy some milk and eggs. She spoke the purest English of the four, and I noticed that she stood with her hands folded in front of her while I was speaking; it was a flattering attitude—it gave the impression that what was being said was of great interest and importance.

We talked a little more and then, accompanied by the

unwilling, horror-struck youth with a hurricane-lamp to show me the way, I carried my eggs and milk up the hill to Hafod.

It was strange that I had not been able to hit the right path; nothing could have been plainer, and at least once on my way down I must have crossed it. I said something of this nature to the youth, choosing easy words and speaking distinctly; but he made no reply. Near the door of Hafod he left me suddenly, with a guttural laugh.

After my supper I pushed the crocks to one side and sat in front of the stove—it was drawing well and I had its doors open. The chair was comfortable, and as I sat there smoking, I had a very real sense of happiness. A good meal and creature comfort after a long and tiring day had something to do with it, but more came from a recollection of that good family down there at the farm. Perhaps it was because my own life had had so little domesticity in it that I appreciated it as much as I did, but I am sure that the most hag-ridden family man would have been affected by the gentle kindness, the fittingness (if decency is too pedantic) of the life of those people as I had seen them that evening. It may be that the lamplight had something to do with the strength of the impression, the lamplight and the glowing fire: an old man cannot look patriarchal under an electric bulb, but in the limited radiance of a lamp the attitudes of people, drawn closer of necessity, have a new significance, and their faces borrow character.

I was not sure of the relationships: at one time during the evening I had thought that the old man was employed by the younger, but at another it seemed that he possessed the farm. The young woman, the lovely young woman Bronwen, was almost certainly the young man's wife, though it was not impossible that she was the old lady's daughter. They had the confusing habit of referring to one another as Mr. Vaughan or Mrs. Vaughan, and as they all shared the same surname this told me nothing. It is true that I had heard the old people called Nain and Taid—grandmother and grandfather—but that might have been no more than the local usage, implying no actual relationship. One thing that was clear was that the youth was the farm servant. They spoke of him as the gwas when they said that he would light me home. He came from a family in the village, also called Vaughan, but not related.

I could have made it all perfectly clear by asking one of them, but that would not have been possible. Apart from their polite questions on how I liked their country they had not, even by implication, asked me anything about myself. That was a remarkable point of breeding, I thought, recalling it, they did not obviously avoid questions; it was that they showed no curiosity. I had not volunteered anything about myself, and as I was going to bed it occurred to me that it was a pity that I had not said anything about my acquaintance with their language. No natural opportunity had arisen, and it would have been absurd to drag in my little smattering all by itself, like a dormouse on a haywain. I wished that I had, because it was obvious that they would have spoken to one another in Welsh before me thinking their words to be private. It is true that, as far as my understanding went, they were; still, the principle remained, and I resolved to set things right at the first occasion that offered.

I did find it a little mortifying, I must admit, to see that I had hardly understood anything at all of the Welsh that I had heard spoken. Two or three words, no more, although for the last few weeks I had been turning over my old note-books. The book language and the spoken Welsh, spoken rapidly, indistinctly and with innumerable contractions and elisions, were hardly recognizable as the same tongue: it was worse for me, because my friend Annwyl had come from Bro Morgannwg, the southernmost limit of the language, and it is well known that there is a great difference between the dialects of the north and the south.

The next day I was busy pottering about, finding where things were and putting my belongings away. I did get out once, to go to Pentref, the village, for tobacco: I had not intended to do this, because I meant to give up smoking, but somehow the arguments in favor of tobacco presented themselves so strongly that I said I would just go down and see whether there was any good brand in the shop.

I had hardly seen anything of the valley when I arrived and although from the time I had woken up I had been looking out of the window and stepping into the garden to stare at my surroundings the low cloud had prevented me from forming any clear impression: so I was not prepared for the splendor that stood high all round when I came out for my walk. The cloud had gone and there was the soaring mass of the Saeth sweeping up into the clear sky. It was a mountain as a child draws a mountain, a sharp, stabbing triangle. I had studied the maps, but the contours and figures, particularly the figures, had deceived me; I had expected hills, little more, and here was a mountain. Its height in figures meant nothing: there was the majesty, the serene isolation, that you expect (if Switzerland is your criterion) only from ten thousand feet and more. Indeed, I have seen many quite well-known peaks, high above the snow-line, without a tenth part of the Saeth's nobility.

There was no snow on the Saeth, of course, but there was something very nearly as striking—great runs of shale, beds of it tilted up to ferocious slopes, and the lines of its fall.

This strong impression of grandeur never faded; the more I saw the mountain the finer I thought it. It was incredibly changeable: on some days it would be a savage, menacing dark mountain, a somber weight—I had almost said a threat—in the sky. Then in the evening, some evenings, when each rock on the skyline was etched hard and distinct against the sky, the Saeth took on a quality of remoteness, almost of unreality. The Saeth in moonlight, like something out of El Greco's mind; the Saeth with snow; the hard triangular peak of the Saeth ripping through the tearing driven clouds from the sea—with a mountain like that outside your window, you are not lonely.

The rest of the valley was in proportion. It lay deep, wide and smooth between its long enclosing ridges and the stream wound through the brilliant green of the water meadows. There was the bottom of the valley, green, and with a narrow long strip of fields; then the lower gentle slopes, still green but with more brown mixed in the color; a long, horizontal wall and then the slopes rose faster, more and more barren, to boulders, shale and at last to the barbarity of naked rock. Everywhere there were walls, dry-stone walls criss-crossing, walls of enormous length, running up impossible slopes. The whitish spots that I saw on the far slope, peppered the length and breadth of it, right up to the top, were sheep; they could be heard, if one stopped to listen, and their voices came from every quarter, drifting on the wind.

There were the farms, with neat squares of wall by them and a few trees: the one I had been to last night was just under me—absurd to have mistaken the way. They had dove-gray roofs that blended with the outcropping rock; one at least I stared at for several minutes before I saw it at all.

Then there was the huge extent of air. I do not know how it is, but this feeling of the air as a thing with dimensions is peculiar to mountainous countries. Between me and the dark curved ridge that closed the top of the valley there was perhaps three miles of air, perfectly clear, but somehow evident. It was keen, fine air, a pleasure to breathe.

I stepped out briskly for the village, fairly glowing with satisfaction. As I went down the road the other mountain, the mountain in whose side Hafod was wedged, began to loom up behind me. Before, I had been too near to see it, too much under the first slopes. It was not until I was right at the village itself that the head of Penmawr rose up. It was a great high-shouldered mountain, with three ragged peaks; higher by a head and shoulders than the Saeth; imposing in its way, but lacking unity, and for dramatic beauty not to compare.

The long quarry road ran up to its lower side and vanished round a shoulder, to reappear much higher and farther away. My little white box showed just under the road; the sun caught the panes of the two front windows.

I did not see the village until I was almost on top of it. It was in a sheltered corry, hidden from our part of the valley by an overgrown series of hillocks that I took to be a glacial moraine. Below this place the identity of the valley changed; it was savage and rocky, but somehow less satisfactory. There was a crossroads; I turned to the right and there was the village a hundred yards from me, across the stream.

It was a shock. I had not expected anything like it. It was a hard, rectilinear pattern, almost a cross, set on the rising slope of the Saeth ridge. The upright of the cross was the shiny macadam road on which I was walking, the cross-piece a lane running about thirty yards each way. In the lower left-hand space in the cross there was an official-looking building in a bald yard, obviously the school. The chapel stood in the right-hand top space. At the intersection I saw the bright red of the post-office.

As I walked into the village, I saw that all the houses were exactly the same. They were built of slate, thick pieces either cut or left ragged, almost black. The windows were edged with yellow brick. The paint on the woodwork was everywhere a dark, purplish chocolate. There were no gardens at all: the houses rose straight from the earth.

Those were my first impressions: they were mistaken. After I had been to the post-office (they had no tobacco; and in a way I was glad, because I was already ashamed of the weakness of my resolution) I walked about a little more and saw that there were four houses out of the pattern; they had front-door steps and railings. I had not noticed them before because they were overwhelmed by the monstrous chapel, which, like them, was covered with yellow stucco. It was a shocking piece of work: I got used to it, in time, but at first it made me gasp. I can hardly describe it; there is not much point, anyhow. It made a few bows in the direction of English church architecture (English church architecture of the '80's) and a few more at each of the classical orders in turn.

The post-office was the only shop; and it did not appear to have much in it—it was not the general store that I had expected.

I wondered what the devil the village was doing there, what was its *raison d'être*. It looked like the outburst of a malignant building lunatic. I was still staring at the chapel when a gentle rain began to fall. At once the gray roofs turned black and the slate walls grew even darker.

I hurried back to avoid a ducking, and as I came to the crossroads I looked at the village again. It was a monstrous thing and it should never have been called a village; but it was not without beauty if you considered the hard lines (harder still now in the rain) and mechanical pattern of stark rectangles and cubes against the unbounded sweep of dissolving mountainside. Still, I was not sorry that it was invisible from Hafod, and that our upper valley was shut clean away from any influence of that kind whatever.

Lloyd

===

"My reason for coming here today, Mr. Lloyd," he said, "is to ask you to tell me about Pentref. We thought about it for some time and decided that there was no one else so well qualified: ministers come and go, and even if they stayed all the time, I do not know that a minister would be able to see the whole picture so well as the schoolmaster."

Mr. Lloyd did not answer at once. It was hard to know where to begin: he knew so much about the place—fifty years of his life—he knew so much that the knowledge turned in unconnected fragments in his head.

"If you were to begin by describing the place?"

"Yes. Yes, I will do my best to describe it."

"Then you might go on to the people."

Mr. Lloyd cleared his throat. "Well, sir, the village—as you know, perhaps—is almost the highest in Gwynedd. It stands in Cwm Bugail, the valley between the Saeth and Penmawr y

Gogledd, about halfway up the valley. The village is not down in the hollow of the valley, because of the floods, but rather up on the slope of the Saeth ridge. The river, it is not more than a stream ordinarily, runs just below the village, by the school, and there is a very old bridge, across it. That is the only old thing in the village, which was built for the big quarry up on Penmawr. It was built by contract in the 1860's, when the slate trade was doing well. The quarry is almost worked out now, but the village is still full—overcrowded it is, indeed: at least, that is my opinion. There are men who still work in the quarry, keeping the pumps in order, and the old quarrymen with silicosis who have pensions, and there are the grown-up children who go to work in Llanfair or Dinas—it is difficult to find houses near their work. There are twenty-one houses: there are some people who do not like the style, but I prefer things squared off and exact rather than straggling. And there is the school and the chapel. The school is large for a village school, big enough for me to have had a female teacher for the infants. It has a good asphalt yard and slate lavatories; you can see the building from far off because of the big green ventilators.

"We were very proud of the chapel. It was built when the men were earning good money—they worked by bargains then—and it was big enough to hold everybody when we had an eisteddfod. No expense had been spared inside, and a carver had come from Liverpool for the woodwork: it is in the Gothic taste inside; the outside is plainer—it is not stucco, but a patent composition.

"The village does lack some things. There are no shops except for the sub-post-office, and no smithy, and the bus does not come nearer than three miles. But there is the telephone, and the air is very healthy. The schoolmaster's house has indoor sanitation and a bath in the scullery.

"Then there are the farms. The upper farms, the ones above the bridge, make a whole with the village; the ones below, except for Cletwr, belong more to Pontyfelin, the village down on the main road. They are much older than the village, of course. Some of them are very old-fashioned, and you find the cattle under the same roof as the people and only the big open fire to cook by and the people sleeping in the half-loft, with no doors, but those farms are in the lower part. In the upper part there are three farms; Hendre on the left, nearest the village, owned by Gwilym Thomas, a little farm with not much mountain; then farther up Hendre Uchaf, John Evans. On the other side is Gelli, which is reckoned the best farm. It has not as much mountain as Hendre Uchaf, but it has more arable at the bottom of the valley, and the mountain it has is sheltered, with good enough pasture for them to run some beasts as well as the sheep.

"There are also two cottages in the upper part of the valley, one on each side, about halfway up. The one on the left is Bwthyn-bach, Megan Bowen's cottage. The other is Hafod; it used to be taken by people for the summer until Mr. Pugh came to live there.

"The other farms by the village and to each side in the valleys next to ours also belong to our community. There are eight—nine if you count Tyddyn Mawr."

"We might leave them to one side for the moment. It is Gelli that interests me particularly."

Lloyd gave him a hesitating look and paused before he went on.

"Well, Gelli was the best farm. It was farmed by Armin

Vaughan. He came from Cwm y Glo when I was a very young man. I had known him before and we were friends, although he was older than me. I always liked him very much; even when he was young he was quiet, sober and respectable. He came of good parents; they were very poor, but they did their best for their children. He was a strong worker and a religious man: everyone liked him. But he was one of those men things go wrong for: however conscientious he was (and no man could have been more conscientious than Armin Vaughan) some accident would come to spoil his work.

"The very first year he came to Gelli some Liverpool people made a picnic fire up by the far barn and burnt all the hay; then it was found that his cousin Ifan had forgotten to post off the insurance. It was still in the pocket of his best coat. Then another time a dog bit a man in his farmyard and he had to pay all the time the man was in hospital, as well as damages. It was always like that for him, as well as the ordinary misfortunes, like black-leg and fluke in the sheep, foxes, blight on the potatoes, rain for the hay and the corn; he had all of them worse than his neighbors.

"He had taken a big farm with almost no money at all after he had paid for the sheep (the sheep were high the year he came, and they have to be paid for, the ewes on the mountain, as soon as you come in) and he needed two or three good years to put him on his feet. He did not have them, though he worked so hard. The sheep went down; it was terrible for all the farmers, even those with money behind them. But he worked and worked and kept going somehow. He was a good man. He was very much respected in the valley.

"His wife was a big help to him. She was very pretty when

she was young; she came from the same part of the country as he did, but I had not known her before she came to our valley.

"They said she was not very great as a housekeeper: however that may be, she was a great help to him. I have seen her early and late, working before the light and after it.

"They did not have a good year until Emyr was born. He was their only child that lived. You would have thought no one had ever had a child before, they were so pleased with him. Things began to go a little better for them after that; not well, but a little better, so they could wind the year round.

"Armin Vaughan worked even harder, with a son to work for. He was a good boy, Emyr; I was fond of him from the start. He came to me at school, of course, and from the beginning he was a good pupil—he was good at Sunday school too, like his father. He was a great improver: I mean he took his lessons with intelligence—I could tell him the principle of things when other boys could only learn examples by rote. There were some boys I liked more although they were not so good, rougher boys like Moses Gwyn and poor John Davies Tŷ-bach, but I was proud of Emyr when the inspector came. Emyr liked me too, and I can give a proof of it: it is a very hard thing to break a boy of the vices that may come on him, and I do not know how it can be done at all unless there is affection on both sides and good spirit in the boy. By break I do not mean just driving the trouble out of sight. Often with my boys I did no more than that, I know, but with Emyr I was more successful. Twice I had to talk to him; once it was about cruelty to a captured bird (it surprised me in him, so tender usually) and once it was about some habits—it is difficult to explain, but they might have grown very unpleasant and dangerous if they had not been corrected before they grew strong and established. I mention this because it shows the confidence between us: he turned from the beginning of this bad way and I never saw any backsliding.

"He was serious as a young fellow; no larking about down to Llan or going with the factory girls at Dinas—indeed I thought that perhaps he was not the marrying kind. The same thought came to his father and mother, and it grieved them; for of course they wanted grandchildren.

"He did marry, however, and at the beginning I was almost sorry when I heard he was keeping company because he had had the idea of following the Institute's agricultural courses, and now it would be all out of his head.

"His young lady was not from our valley; she lived over in Cwm Priddlyd, behind Llanfihangel. It would be a good thing for Emyr, everybody said, because her father owned the farm of Cwm Priddlyd, and even if her brother Meurig married, Bronwen would still have an interest in it. Armin Vaughan was all for it, and so was old Mrs. Vaughan. They both wanted the very best for Emyr (it was a pity for him they loved him quite so much, I thought) and Armin Vaughan's father had worked at Cwm Priddlyd, so they knew everything about the land there—a small farm; but very good, and with fine buildings. And Bronwen was the only girl Emyr had ever looked at, so they wanted to close it quickly. Then Bronwen was very well brought up and a good worker: she was Church, like her mother, but thinking of the farm and of Emyr they did not mind that. Most of all they wanted grandchildren, soon.

"It was not my place to say anything against it, in any sort of way, and when they asked me about him I gave him the best character I have ever given a young man.

"Well, they were married and he brought her home to Cwm Bugail. I was going down to stay with my cousin William Edwards at Swansea, so I only saw her arrive and then I was away. By the time I was back she was quite established. I had taken away what you might call a neutral impression: everybody was happy, there was singing and laughing, and Bronwen was very pretty, but still I was not altogether pleased with the marriage, and I never have approved of living two generations together. And there was something about the girl—she was not our sort. I do not know how I decided it, or what I disliked about her, but there it was.

"When I came back they told me in the village that Bronwen Vaughan, Gelli, was proud. I do not know how she had made herself unpopular; she was always pleasant to the women who went there as far as I could learn, but unpopular she was with most of the village people. Her not coming to chapel had something to do with it, no doubt, and I think there was something in what I shall try to explain. The Vaughans were doing quite well now and some other people were not; Emyr had much better luck as a farmer than his father, and he had a better head. There was a certain amount of jealousy because of that, and people not liking to say anything against Emyr or Armin Vaughan said it, or felt it, against Bronwen.

"In a little while too I heard many other unfavorable things: I do not remember them in detail, but the sum was that Bronwen had brought too many fine things with her, and she was too high to talk in the shop at Pentref, and she was not as kind as she should be to the old people. I do not know how much there was to all this at that time, and I must say that whenever I saw Mrs. Emyr she was always polite to me in her way, and whenever I went there she made me welcome.

"People grew more used to her in time, and liked her more I believe: at least I did not hear the remarks that had been so frequent. The women took to her more when she had her baby, and then, when she was more tied, I suppose, she left off going all the way down to the church and came to our chapel sometimes, which brought her more into the ordinary life of the valley. But then again, as the boy began to grow she offended people once more by wanting to bring him up in her own fashion. She had strong ideas. People said they were fancy. They may have been very well, for all I know, but they were not her mother-in-law's ideas, nor the ideas of our valley.

"Nothing that was ever said against her came from the old people. Nobody heard Emyr's mother say a word until the beginning of the disagreement about the child, and even then it was only a very little to a close friend.

"Emyr, as far as I could see, was quite happy. He was working very hard on the farm now that his father was older, and I saw less of him than I used to, by far, so I cannot speak very well of that time.

"Another reason that comes to my mind for her un-popularity at the beginning was her sister-in-law Meurig's wife. They had no children, and they were well-off for mountain farmers, with no rent to pay and the good land they had. She was a little, sharp, black sparking woman, fond of dress: her voice, a high, loud soprano, had been trained when she was young (she was rather older than Meurig, and quite fifteen years older than Bronwen) and in chapel she sang half a note in front of the other women. She had lived with her parents in Liverpool, and although she spoke perfectly good Welsh (an ugly South Caernarvon accent she had) she pretended not to know a word every now and then, and used an English one instead. She had a way of looking round when she got into a house, looking sharply at the furniture and other things; and at Mary Owen's she dusted her seat before she sat down. Anyone could see that she and Bronwen did not like one another, but there were many people who blamed the family, and Bronwen as one of them."

"I see," said the other. "Thank you very much; now I have a clearer picture of the background. This brings us up to the time with which I am principally concerned. I should be glad if you would tell me about the cottage you have mentioned, and Mr. Pugh, who took it."

"Hafod, the cottage, is on the quarry road, above Gelli. It is only a very small, old-fashioned place, but summer visitors liked it and took it almost every year. Mr. Pugh took it at the end of one summer. I heard that he was an English gentleman from Oxford; I did not learn exactly what he did there, but I understood he was a tutor at the university. At that time I did not see him, except in the village, but I heard all about him.

"I was surprised to hear that he had taken it permanently the next year and that he was going to live there all the time, winter and summer."

"Why were you surprised?"

"He seemed too young to retire, and anyhow, it was only a summer place for his sort. It seemed a queer thing for a man to do. I thought perhaps there was something funny about him, but Armin Vaughan said he thought he was a good man. That was at the beginning.

"I met him there one evening—at Gelli, I mean—and we had some talk. I invited him to my house, and I went to his; but I am afraid I was not grand enough for him, and I did not see very much of him. I thought he was quite a respectable gentleman, but I did not like his airs. I know I am only a plain man, but I am B.A. and I know something about my country, so I do not like to be told I am wrong when I am right. Oxford is a very fine place, and a very respectable place, I am sure, but that is not to say that every man who comes from there knows everything. A village schoolmaster may know better *sometimes* indeed.

"Yes, I must say I did not like his airs, though I did not take it seriously then, and it was always Good day, Mr. Lloyd, Good day, Mr. Pugh, when we met in the village or in Llan. But I did not go and push myself on him; it would not have been right, even if I had liked his airs, me being so much an older man, and with a certain position in the neighborhood, and he did not come to see me. It was not until he fell ill in the autumn and was taken down to Gelli that I saw much of him. I visited him when he was ill, and when my cousin Pritchard Ellis, the well-known preacher, came to stay there I often went in the evenings to hear them talk. This was when Mr. Pugh was better again but was still lodging at Gelli.

"It was a real pleasure to hear them talk. I did not like him very much then, but I admired the flow of language he had, and certainly he was very well informed: of course, he had no chance with Pritchard Ellis, the best talker I have ever heard, in Welsh or English. It did give me a kind of satisfaction, too,

to hear him worsted: it showed we could stand up for ourselves in Wales, even without all the advantages. Once or
twice he seemed to get the better of it, but Pritchard explained to me afterwards why this was; and once he became
really violent about some political argument—I was not at-
tending—and the discussion had to be stopped. No; in general he had no chance against Pritchard Ellis.

"Well, that was my opinion of Mr. Pugh at that time. I did
not care for him, nor did Pritchard, but he seemed to be an
honest, respectable, quiet man, though proud and con-
ceited."

Pugh

T hat spring my uncle Caley, the lawyer, died: I had not
seen him for twenty years and I had never liked him (an
angry starched white prig) any more than he liked me, so I
was not much affected by his death. However, he died intestate: I was his heir-at-law, and I felt a certain compunction in
taking his money—he would so have disliked my having it.
He was not a real uncle, but a cousin of the older genera-
tion.

It did not take me long to overcome these scruples. No
one else would naturally have benefited: Bernard was two or
three degrees farther removed than myself, and although he
always cried poverty he ran two cars and hung gee-gaws on
his enormous wife until she looked like a Christmas tree. It
was not really worth mentioning this; my compunction had
vanished before the next post, but I felt that it was creditable
in so poor a man to have entertained it so long.

To resume: my uncle Caley died intestate, and I inherited. The first firm decision that came into my mind was to take Hafod and go and live in it. I would buy it if it was for sale or lease it if it were not, but at all events I would go and live there. I could now. Often, during my stay in the autumn I had said that if I searched a hundred years I should never chance on a place I liked more, and I had reckoned the number of years before I could retire: it was not the effect of first acquaintance or enthusiasm; I had been there long enough to see the disadvantages, but even if they had been doubled or trebled I should still have been of the same opinion.

All through the winter I had thought of the cottage (I used to draw it in idle moments) and the valley and the good Vaughans at the farm. I had sent them a Christmas card, and I had intended to send the child a present, but I left it too late and could find nothing suitable.

But now I could go there: the faint, ultimately-to-be-realized-perhaps dreams with which I had nourished myself in the winter—a garden, drainage, a bathroom—took on an immediate concrete reality. That was my one basic decision. A great many other things occurred to me, minor things; I was tempted by books, a piano and a car. I hesitated a long time over the car, and I believe that I would have bought it, if I had known how to drive.

It was not really such a great deal of money; but up to that time I had never had a hundred pounds, clear, unmortgaged and expendable, in my hands at one time, so a sum of thousands appeared a great deal to me. The solicitor who acted for me referred to it as This little nest-egg, and showed me how, by careful investment it could be made to produce an income a little larger than that which I earned. He said it would be very useful as extra pocket-money; perhaps he meant it as a joke: it irritated me beyond words.

For me it was a release. I had spent many happy days in my college, and there were many men I knew and liked in the university. But I was unsuited for my teaching duties; I performed them badly and with a great deal of pain, and to the end I could never stand up to lecture without dying a little private agony. And in recent years some of the men who had come into the college were not of the kind that I could like; they joined with one or two of the older fellows and the bursar to make what old Foley called "a corporate platitude and an underbred aggressive commonplace."

But with all these strong feelings (and I see that I have painted them rather larger than life), feelings that were profound more than vivid, I found my actual separation from my college much more painful than I had expected. Very painful: not merely twice or three times as painful but hundreds of times. My friends, they were so unexpectedly kind, but even more my—not exactly enemies, but the people to whom I was, in general, little more than civil, came up to me and said the most obliging things, and with a sincerity that I found very moving indeed. It was coals of fire, and often I was heartily ashamed of the feelings that I had entertained and the witticisms that I had made in petto.

There was a presentation, speeches, and some good wine. They saw me off handsomely. My last sentimental pilgrimage and my last night in my old rooms cost me some hard tears.

It was not a transient feeling: when I was sitting in the train it seemed to me that the disadvantages of a collegiate life had never been so slight, and never again could I recapture the strength of my dislike for it.

I had hoped that Wales would compensate me for my sacrifice, but at Ruabon it was raining, and from there a dirty little train crawled spasmodically through cloud and showers, threading its interminable way through the invisible Principality. In the end I missed my station and I had all the difficulty in the world to find a cab that would take me from Llanfair up Cwm Bugail.

When I reached my own house through the pouring rain it was dark and the fires had not been lighted: a tomb-like smell met me as I opened the door. The old woman from across the valley had either not received my note or had misunderstood it. I went straight to my damp bed and lay there shivering for an hour or two before I drifted off to a haunted sleep. It was a fitting end for a day that had begun with emotional exhaustion and had ended in extreme physical fatigue.

Things looked much better in the morning. The sun was shining from a brilliant sky and the valley was looking finer than I had ever seen it. From my bed I looked straight out over to the other side, where the ridge of the Saeth sloped up right-handed to fill half my window. By moving a little I could see the peak itself, rising above a wisp of cloud like a veil, still just tinged with pink.

The valley was full of lambs. Their voices were everywhere, loud and insistent, a hundred different tones; and everywhere the answering ewes, much deeper. I could see the lambs on the other side. So far away they were no more than white flecks, but brilliant white, and never still.

Quite suddenly I felt active and happy, and I longed to be

out. The air smelled wonderful in the garden, and there was a bird of some kind singing away, as I should have sung if I could. The boy from the farm appeared: he lurked about in view for some time and then shouted something in which I caught the word Parcels, and he pointed down to the farm. I went down and found that the kind people had taken in a number of things that I had sent to Hafod—household things and books, gramophone, records and so on—and had carefully stored them out of the rain. They were as welcoming as if I had been a native returning—how very pleasant it is to be made cordially welcome—and they insisted on giving me breakfast, ham of their own curing, eggs, a mountain of butter, and their own bread. Afterwards young Vaughan picked up my cases as though they were empty (I can think of nothing heavier nor more awkward than a box of gramophone records) and carried them up the hill to Hafod.

For the next week I hardly stirred from the cottage. It is unusual, perhaps, for a man to reach middle age without ever having set up house; but I had not. It was terribly hard work: when one is naturally unhandy and has to learn all the techniques for the first time the putting up of a single shelf is a day's labor; but Lord, the satisfaction of putting the books on it, clearing the floor of them and their packing, stowing away the boxes and reducing the place to something like order. There is a wonderful satisfaction, a feeling of accomplishment when you sit down for the first time in a neat room and look at the straight rows, one above another to the ceiling, all standing square on solid bases. Without being a bibliomaniac it has always seemed to me that books are the supreme decoration of a room, and I took the liveliest pleasure in arranging them according to their height and color.

I had a great disappointment, however; it was the defection of Mrs. Bowen, who was to do for me. It was a blow, for I had based my assumptions, my projected way of life on somebody else doing the cooking and the work of the household. She was a savage old creature, with rather less notion than myself about the running of a house, but I had taken a liking to her in the autumn, and I had hoped that she might get better with practice. It was an extravagant hope, as I should have known from the visits I paid her: her place was spick and span outside (she was a great gardener) but the interior, as much as could be seen of it in the gloom, was a congestion of huge vases, rococo furniture and tin trunks ajar. Most of these objects still had their lot numbers: the old lady had a passion for auctions, and attended every sale within twenty miles. She knew the mountain paths like a shepherd, and she could be seen in the wild desolation of the Diffwys creeping along bowed under a crimson pouffe or even, as I found her once, recruiting her strength on an Empire buffet, poised on the black crag above the silent, menacing Llyn Du.

She was quite well off, with pensions for her two men who had been killed in the quarry. It was surprising to hear that she had been married; I had supposed her to be one of those strong-minded, masculine women who do not marry but live alone, self-contained and formidable, to the end of their days. Her needs were few; twenty pounds would probably have covered her yearly expenditure apart from the auctions, and people gave her things, mutton and pork after a slaughtering, black pudding, corn for her hens. In the season she went to every farm for the shearing, where she was an expert roller of fleeces. She worked hard when she chose to work, but it was more from habit than from interest in the wages, and to satisfy her curiosity and her need for conversation. I know it was not for money that she threaded the mountains at shearing time, because she always took a fleece as her day's pay, as they used to do in former times; but instead of having it made into flannel as the old people did she stored the wool in her loft, where it mounted and mounted, the home of innumerable rats and mice. Moldering wool was the chief of the smells in her cottage; the next in strength was her goat, her companion and pet.

The first time I went to ask why she had not come she gave me a cup of tea with her goat's milk in it; even in that dim light I could see the encrusted grime on the mug. There was something soft at the bottom, which my spoon encountered but did not entirely dislodge.

It was conversation that proved the downfall of our relation; that and wounded pride. She was the most garrulous old woman I have ever heard. She knew very little English, but that did not prevent her from starting to talk as soon as she opened my door, a flood of words that did not stop until she closed the door behind her. As far as I could make out they were mostly anecdotes of her young days, or the history of families living in the valley, diseases, catastrophe, anger and death. It was impossible to follow her. Most of the farming people had some trouble with English pronouns (*hi* in Welsh is *she* in English, which starts them off on the wrong foot) but none was so wild as this old lady.

I used to listen with strained attention to such phrases as "Then it went off with the *hwnna* [this took the place of any unknown English word] with Dai to the sheeps; and tomorning I say 'Men: the damned things.' " It was a pity that I could not understand her, for I am sure she would have been most interesting: I tried, but the difficulty of language was far from being the greatest barrier. Her mental processes were tortuous and involved; she was the victim of association. She would plunge into a vast series of parentheses and never come out. An account of Criccieth fair thirty years ago would become the history of Mr. Williams, Moelgwyn, and then by some fresh association, dark to me, it would turn to a tale of obscure injustice.

In the end I stopped trying, and she resented it. Once, during an inordinately tedious speech I got up at the end of a paragraph, hoping to be allowed to get on with the book that lay open on the table, but she said, "Sit down. I am not finishing . . ." so firmly that I had no choice.

She grew more and more irregular in her attendance as I listened to her less, although I tried to make up for it by paying her more than our bargain. I wrote to her once or twice, to ask her to order coal if she were going down to Dinas, or to come on Thursday instead of Friday. She never acted on these notes, and answered evasively if I asked her about them: it occurred to me that she might not understand written English, so one day I wrote to her in Welsh. She never came again after that. She was quite illiterate (I wish I had known: I would not have humiliated her for the world) and she could make nothing of any of the notes; but when she learned that the last was in Welsh she found it wounding and insulting. She forgave me in the end, and we were quite friendly, but she said she was too old to go out any more.

I looked everywhere for another woman; I advertised and made inquiries as far as Llanfair and Dinas, but there was none to be found. There was no middling gentry in this part of the country, and no local tradition of going out to service.

I was obliged to keep house for myself. I did not do so badly after a while, though the ordinary mechanical operations like washing up, or making a bed always took me very much longer than they would have taken a woman. In a way it was a good thing: it opened a new perspective to me. Formerly I had used what I now found to be an unreasonable number of plates, cups and saucers, knives and forks: when each of these things has to be washed up, dried and put away, things take on a different aspect. Now I grew careful of my saucer (a triumph if it remained unslopped), never put butter or marmalade on the edge of my plate, so that the plate might get by with no more than a few crumbs, which could be blown off, and I learned that one course to each meal was enough.

My simple diet appeared to suit me. That, the change, the excitement, the unwonted exercise and the mountain air combined in the first few months to make me feel better than I had felt for years. I ate when I chose and as much or as little as I chose—a great change from the set, unvarying meals of my former life. I rather insist upon this point, because I am convinced that a man's diet and his surroundings have a deep effect on him. Before this time I had tended to coddle myself: I was hagridden by an ignominious and painful digestive trouble, and in an exactly ordered life I had spent much too much time watching my symptoms and worrying about them. My new way of eating did not have the permanent good effect that I had hoped (I write like a hypochondriac) but the vast country opened and strengthened my being in ways that I had never imagined. Many things that had appeared all-important dwindled to trifles, and other values rose. It is difficult to explain because it is difficult to seize; but I know that I began to feel more of a man—more complete and masculine—and less like a neutral creature in an unsatisfactory body.

The strength of the country; that was a new concept for me. I had known the Cotswolds fairly well, and the Sussex downs; they are very beautiful, but they had never given me this idea of strength—a direct and powerful influence. This was something quite different: from my very first days in the valley it struck me that men, here, were no longer in the majority; it was the untamed land. It is possible that I exaggerated this because of my urban background, but making all allowances, it still seemed to me that it was neither fanciful nor weak to feel that the ancient order was hardly disturbed here. (If this was the case, and I am sure it was, a man's natural reaction would be to become more virile.)

The ancient order was hardly disturbed, particularly at night. I remember standing just under the black precipice that rushes up to the top of the Saeth looking down at the three or four handkerchiefs of fields down in the bottom of the valley and comparing their extent with the prodigious sweep of untouched mountain; the night was touching on the barren land, making it vaster and more powerful, while the little fields dwindled and vanished.

There was no longer that great buffer of civilization between a man and his remote origins: I felt it strongly; and in an attempt to convey something of what I mean I have written the two following pieces, although they break the run of my narrative.

I was walking along the road in the morning of a beautiful

gentle day when I met Emyr Vaughan going the round of his sheep. We were well acquainted and friendly by this time and he often used to take me part of the way with him to show me things and explain them. It was still the lambing season, and twice every day he went clean round the lower mountain. He was having trouble this year with weak ewes who could not feed their lambs, and with foxes. As we walked he showed me here and there a patch of skin with the close-curled wool of a new lamb on it, and once the hoof, or the foot, of a lamb with the shank still uneaten. He slackened his pace for me, but it was still an effort to keep up, and I did not always hear or understand what he said; however, I remember being struck again by the extraordinary way he recognized individual sheep. "That ewe there, she is the daughter of the one by the wall. She had twins, but she could not feed both of them, and I put one to that ewe we passed by the road, the one I said had the maggot very bad last year—her lamb had the brait." It was obvious that he was not talking for effect: he had hundreds of sheep there, and he knew each one, with its maternal ancestry. I do not think that any of them had names except those few who had been hand-reared at the farm, brought up with a bottle, and I meant to ask him how he identified each, whether he said inwardly, "There is that sheep with the drooping ears and brown legs, the daughter of the one who got caught in the trap the autumn before the bad winter."

We were coming down again to the road a little way above my cottage when we found the body of a lamb, dragged between two rocks. Its head was eaten off.

"Diwch annwyl!" he said. It was a fine well-grown lamb. He said that he thought he had seen the mother earlier in

the day, much farther up. It was a fox of course, he said, and when he had thought for some time he said, "I will put some poison to it tonight." He spoke with an air of caution—a hushed cunning, as if it were something illegal. He said he was sure I would not tell anybody. It was when he spoke like this that he lost his amiability entirely; all the idiot sharpness of the peasant came into his face; it was as if his eyes diminished and went red round the edges.

I left him shortly after this and went home to make myself a pot of coffee and to cut some sandwiches for my lunch; the day was so fine that I decided to explore the Diffwys, the land that lay up above the end of the valley on the northern side.

If I have managed to give a clear impression of Cwm Bugail it will be remembered that on the left-hand side is a green path that runs across the face of the Saeth and up toward a high cleft at the junction of the mountain's shoulder and the hemicycle of rock that closes the top of the valley. A stream comes down from this cleft in a series of falls—a magnificent spectacle after a few days of rain—and the cleft itself is the beginning of the country that I wanted to explore. The green path—it soon stopped being green and turned to shale, but all that I saw from my window was green, and I always thought of it as the green path—took me longer than I had expected, with the sun on my back and my heavy coat too hot. With pauses I do not suppose that I spent less than two hours reaching the top. It was worth pausing often; every time I turned there was more of the world spread below under me, and more visible over the Penmawr ridge, and all from a higher, more detached and god-like standpoint. It is good for one's self-esteem to be high up.

At the cleft, a dramatically narrow and decisive entrance

to the unknown high country, I turned for a last look down the length of Cwm Bugail: my cottage was there, distinct because of its whitewash, absurdly small, smaller than a matchbox, and the whole vast extent of the air was lit with the sun. Past the corner, through the black rocks of the cleft and at once it was another world, a sunless chasm with a silent lake. Chasm is not the right word; one thinks of a chasm from above, an enormous crack going *down*, essentially down. In this narrow, deep valley I was at the bottom, looking up. On my left hand the side was sheer, nearly the whole length of it; a precipitous scree here and there, and sometimes a little heather, but mostly naked rock going straight up to the top of the Saeth: the bed of the valley was a tarn, black, shining water with an abrupt and barren edge— no reeds, no mud, nothing green at all; it changed harshly from naked water to naked rock. On the right the land rose in a steep slope, a shapeless, tormented moorland with bare rock showing, neither so high nor so sheer as the wall on the left, but still reaching halfway up the sky. There was no breath of wind to stir the top of the water, and in all the length of the valley I could see no thing alive, nor in the air above it.

From the run of the valley and the disposition of the soaring black cliff on its southern side the sun could never come into it at any time. At first, panting from my climb, I found the coolness agreeable, but after a little while I began to feel cold, and buttoned my jacket.

A sheep track ran along before me, and I decided that I would try to walk round the lake before having my sandwiches: it seemed pointless to carry them too (they were bulky in my pocket and had galled me all the way up the

green path) so I put them on a convenient rock, with the
intention of coming back to sit there and eat them after I
had been round the lake. Before I left I looked around in
order to be sure that I should find them again, and my eye
was caught by a shape on the skyline—a skyline that I had to
lean back to see at all. Right up there on the edge of the
black precipice there was this thing, perched like a gargoyle
peering down. I could not tell why it had caught my eye:
there were hundreds of jutting, strangely-shaped rocks all
along that weathered salient, and none had fixed my attention. However, it did catch my eye, and held it. I could not
see what it was: a sheep, perhaps? These agile mountain
sheep did take up the most extraordinary attitudes, poised
on an overhanging rock with a handful of grass in its crev-
ices. Or conceivably one of those wild goats that I had heard
about? It was a strange way for a sheep to stand, hooked
there.

I suppose, from the comparisons I made at the time with a
sheep or a goat, that the thing was lighter in color than the
surrounding rock: I do not remember now. What I do recall,
and most clearly, is the air that it had of *crouching* there,
poised over the valley. It was, of course, merely fanciful to
suppose a malignance in it, a sort of evil domination of all
that it looked down upon. It was fanciful, of course, and
outside that sterile place it seems even absurd; but those
were the ideas that came to me.

In the end I said that whether it was a sheep or a rock or a
goat it did not greatly matter, and set off along the track.
From the far end of the valley (Cwm Erchyll was its name) I
had over-simplified its construction; here and there I found
a bay with a little sad gray beach of pebbles, and at the end

there was a bog with a living stream flowing through it to fill the lake. Here a small bird like a snipe got up at my feet and stopped my heart dead still; it winged low over the water, a white flash in its flight and the saddest heartbroken cry in the world.

Where the bog and the lake merged the shore was black and there were rushes: the stream ran cutting deep between banks of a spongy black substance, and in some places I could hear the sound of invisible tributaries that ran underground. On the shore itself the firm black mud showed a line of footprints; they looked to me like those of a dog, but a fox was more likely. It struck me again, and more forcibly, that a man can be ignorant of an infinite number of important, everyday things and still be reckoned educated. In this instance I could not distinguish between the tracks of a dog and a fox; it was not important, perhaps, but it was typical: I had not known the name of that melancholy bird, nor the curious plants that stood in the bog-pool before me—I did not know their names, still less their qualities. A hundred other cases presented themselves—the milking of a cow, the difference between a bull and a bullock, the lighting of a fire without kerosene—none perhaps a matter of life and death, but in all amounting to a great shameful fog of ignorance.

These reflections occupied me until I was halfway round the other side of the lake, and there, where I had to negotiate a difficult piece of smooth rock overhanging the water, something prompted me to look up to the top of the black cliff: it was still there, its aspect slightly changed by my change in position, but surely motionless, and a rock without any sort of doubt. This was comforting, I hardly know why, and I crossed the rock and finished my tour of the lake in much higher spirits. When I sat down to my sandwiches I felt positively merry—a glance upwards showed it there, of course, an insignificant rock, though curious. When I had finished my sandwiches it was gone.

I left the tarn with a mind disturbed, more disturbed than I should have believed possible, and turned at the black cleft into our own valley with a feeling of escape and strong relief. The sun was low now, and the shadow was halfway up the Penmawr ridge; the light was much more golden than I remembered to have seen it before—the contrast, perhaps, between the dark, closed country that I had just left and this wide, beautiful valley with the tawny flank of Penmawr on the other side throwing back a flood of light. There were the white spots of sheep, and down at the bottom the squared fields and the farms with their domestic trees: I had thought of it as wild and barren before, but now, at least for the moment, it looked almost homely.

I went down the green path as slowly as I had come up it; a continual downhill walk that threatens every moment to break into an involuntary run is as tiring as a climb: the sun had left the top of the mountain long before I was halfway down. There was no reason to hurry; the long twilight was as soft as midsummer, and as I went down the length of the mountain wall the stones gave out a gentle warmth. I sat on the bridge for a long while before starting my climb home. The farm was asleep when I passed, walking softly through the yard; only one dog barked, and that perfunctorily—they were getting used to me.

The last steep stretch was very tiring; I had gone too far for one day, and three times on the path up from the farm I stopped to breathe. The third time was just at the corner before my own wall, by the telegraph post: I leaned against it, listening to the singing in the wires, with the gentle breeze on my face and the faint stars showing above the ridge. On the white road, above the cattle-trap, two dogs came trotting toward Hafod. Whose dogs could those be? I thought, and I saw that they were not dogs; they were foxes. They came on steadily; from the road they looked over the low wall into my garden, twice. For a little while they were hidden by the cottage and when they appeared again they were just above me—I could have lobbed a stone underhand beyond them. One was larger than the other—a dog fox and a vixen, I supposed. Astonishing, the length of their legs, the height they stood off the ground. They went a little farther up— they were on my left hand by now—and stopped at the edge of the road, at the curve, where it is built up four or five feet. I thought they must see me now, but if they did they did not care: the smaller one leaned crouching over the edge of the road and screamed out a shrieking howl, horrifyingly loud and daunting. I saw the gape of her jaws. Instantly all the dogs in the valley answered, a furious bawling from each of the farms and a battering against the stable door down in Gelli. The vixen listened, crouching there in her ugly, evil attitude, and as the noise slackened she screamed again. What can give an impression of the sound? An evil, maniac laughter, a triumphant threatening, they were both in it, and something hellish, too.

The dog fox barked once. He too looked out over the valley, and the two stared there like masters in their own place: that was the dominant impression. *They* were the ones.

After a moment they crossed the road back to the smooth

green piece on the far side and I heard them playing with the lamb's foot there. Playing, if playing is the word, for what they did with such a hideous undertone of noise. Once or twice they appeared on the road, worrying and tearing the foot or a piece of wolly skin; then they were gone—they went up the mountain-side and the slope hid them.

At home I went to bed very soon, after a scrap meal, for I was quite done up. But I could not sleep; my legs kept twitching and my mind ran on those appalling foxes. I had never thought of a fox before except as something people hunted, or as the subject of proverbs about cunning: nothing in my vague preconception had given me a hint of that cold, malignant ferocity; I had had no idea of an animal of such a size, such moral dimensions.

When I did sleep it seemed that I had not been off for more than a few minutes before I was awake again, wholly awake, with a feeling of nightmare. It was the yelling of a soul in torment just outside the cottage, a shocking, naked screaming. Instantly young Vaughan's words about the poison came into my mind, and at once I was sure that the fox, or perhaps a loose dog, had returned to the lamb and was now howling out its life in agony. I hurried on my clothes and ran up the road, in the silent, unearthly light of the moon, to the green slope where the lamb lay dragged between the rocks. It was untouched, at least by a fox. Vaughan had gone to it, and what I had heard was the raging vented spite of the vixen forestalled.

I had meant, in writing this, to illustrate my point and to give something of that feeling of strangeness that was always present; not merely to describe two particular incidents. It was a feeling that was with me all the time, more or less consciously; it changed my outlook in many ways that I recognized, and probably in many more that I did not. It is such an intangible thing, the real difference between living in a city and in the wild, untamed country; it is not just the difference of landscape or amenity, it is not that the thunder of a lorry will wake you in the one and the scream of a vixen in the other. It is something subtle and penetrating, and it seemed to me that the only way I could convey anything of it was by example.

Pugh

It is with design that I have not spoken about her yet. At
first I saw little of her, and apart from thinking that it was
strange and pleasant that there should be such a beautiful
woman at the farm, I did not take much notice.

It was in the spring and the summer that it began. I was
settled and established in Hafod and I was going out much
more; young Vaughan had begun my education as a coun-
tryman and I was often on the mountain with him. In the
evenings I went down, sometimes, to ask him about things
that I had seen in the day.

It was then, in those quiet evenings at the farm, that I
began to look at her with particular attention: it was not
because of any sudden emotion but because of something
that I could not quite understand. She had, more than anybody I had ever seen, the appearance of an amiable young
woman, kind and dutiful; and yet day after day I saw the old

lady, Emyr's mother, carrying the pig-swill, scrubbing the floor, drawing the water: sometimes she would have both hands full while the young people were doing nothing. Their standards were different, I knew that: on a mountain farm everybody works—it is hard labor for life. But still this seemed to me to be wrong. There were other less tangible things and I began to wonder whether Bronwen, though lovely to see, were not hard and insensitive; spoilt. A really beautiful face is so rare that one cannot always see beyond it. She certainly tended to be less indulgent than other country-women with her child, an unattractive little boy called Gerallt. There seemed to be a contradiction there: I had no pretensions as a physiognomist, but I was unwilling to believe that I could be as mistaken as that. I am sure that what one calls a good-looking face is the outward expression of a kind and generous spirit: that is why one calls it good. It is the product of experience, as simple as recognizing the fruit by its skin: the appearance that one learns to associate with ripeness is a good appearance. If a peach were at its best when it was as rotten as a medlar, one would soon find a dark, wrinkled peach good-looking. I could have sworn that the goodness in Bronwen's face, the goodness that was there together with her beauty, could not exist with the hardness that appeared in her conduct to old Mrs. Vaughan and, sometimes, to her husband. I thought about it a good deal.

I watched them. I wanted to find that Bronwen was as beautiful as she looked, because when I looked at her I felt a strange, happy feeling—benign, tender—I do not know how to describe it.

I should very much like to describe her, but what is there to say? She was rather less than my height, slim of course, and she looked taller than she was because she was so straight. Her hair was black, black as hair can be, with a deep luster; it was straight. Her face was pale—nothing pink and white about it, and I should have said olive, but for its extraordinary purity. There is a head of one of the Pharaohs in the British Museum: it has a full, serene mouth and eyes, the lines simplified as if they were drawn. It was the same with her, the great wide eyes and her mouth the same: in both it was the line that counted and the pure planes; and with her there was the living color.

That was her in rest, but there was so much as well; the spring of her back, the lovely poise of her head, the way she moved, the timbre of her voice. It is no good—that or a list of virtues.

I was very simple, I suppose. I had no idea that I was there at all until I was in love so deep that it was a pain in my heart. I had thought it was the pleasure of looking at her, the pleasure of joining that good and kind family circle (good in spite of the bad undercurrent that I suspected) and talking about country things with Emyr and the old man. Then one day it was upon me. I knew then what was the matter, and why nothing had seemed profitable but the evenings I spent there; she came in, just as I had seen her the first time, and my heart leaped up and I knew that Emyr was talking but I could not link his words together.

I left soon after. I was afraid of giving myself away; though perhaps I had been gaping at her like a moon-calf for weeks before.

There may be things more absurd than a middle-aged man in the grip of a high-flung romantic passion: a boy can behave more foolishly, but at least in him it is natural.

I kept away. I read Burton and walked the mountains. We had a spell of idyllic weather, and the soft loving wind was a torment to me.

I would not pass those days again. I knew I was a ludicrous figure, and it hurt all the more. I did not eat. I could not read, I could not sleep. I walked and walked, and when one day I broke a tooth on a fruit stone I welcomed the pain.

Long before I had engaged to help with the yearly gathering of the sheep for the shearing, and now the time came round. The boy came up to ask if I would meet Emyr on the quarry road early the next morning. I wondered how I should face him, but there was nothing for it and I said I should be very glad.

He was there in the gray morning, surrounded by his dogs. He was anxious and preoccupied: this was the most important day in the farming year for him and he was afraid it was going to be spoiled by the low-hanging cloud that hid the top half of the mountains. We did not talk much as we went up the road. It was just as well, because I could not make my voice sound natural; even the most trivial words sounded forced and overdone: I wondered that he did not notice it.

As we climbed higher we reached the cloud. It blew in irregular wisps between us and the higher rocks: they would appear, gaunt, outlined dramatically against the streaming cloud behind them, and then vanish.

The aim of the morning's work was to gather all the sheep scattered on the mountain and to drive them down to be shorn. Already a dozen of the other farmers had set out for prearranged points on the limit of the mountain, to be ready at a given hour to start driving the sheep inwards to the gathering place. This was a co-operative task, like the threshing, and some of the farmers came from miles away.

The wind increased as the sun mounted, and before we had reached the top of the road the last streams of cloud had been torn off the round top of Penmawr. Emyr's mind grew lighter: he explained to me that these shearing days were fixed long before at a farmer's meeting, and that if the day turned out rainy (a wet sheep cannot be shorn) or cloudy, so that the sheep cannot be gathered, there is no help for it; the day is lost, and the farm must wait until all the others have had their turn, and then the whole business of the year is unsettled. And the great preparation is wasted: there are perhaps twenty shearers to be fed (friends, neighbors, relations—there are no men to be hired) apart from the hangers-on, and it is a great point of honor among the farms to feed them well. A good wether is killed, a whole ham cut up, innumerable puddings made—a hundred preparations that go to waste if there is no one there to eat them.

However, the cloud had lifted, and it did not look as if it were going to rain. I was posted at a place where the sheep had a habit of plunging down the scree and breaking back into the mountain when they were driven: I was to head them to the pens at the top of the road.

A long wait alone in the cold wind: I allowed fantasies to take shape in my mind and when the first sheep appeared I was not ready for them. They were trotting uneasily toward my gap. Already they were quite close: when I came from the shelter of my rock, shouting and waving my stick to send them back, I was on their flank; the foremost bolted for the gap and the others followed him, rushing along with quick, springing bounces so near past me that I could have struck the last.

This was very bad. I hoped that no one had seen me. Other sheep began to come over the skyline, white strings of a dozen ewes and their lambs. It was easy enough to deal with them if they saw me early enough, but twice a lamb came suddenly through the rocks at my side, bolted down the gap, and then the ewe would follow whatever I might do.

There were more and more: they were coming from new directions now, as the other drivers got nearer to the gathering place. I saw the first of the dogs, and some minutes later the men began to show on the skyline, scattered all along the edge above me. There was a last flurry of warding off the sheep and then abler men with dogs took over my place and the sheep, milling hundreds of them now, were urged into the labyrinth of stone pens at the head of the road.

As I walked down by myself, behind the ordered flock, I realized that these last hours, while I had been herding in the gap, were the first that I had spent without pain for Bronwen since that night—so long ago it seemed.

Down at the farm, with the sheep penned in the yard, my place was not with the shearers: it takes natural dexterity and years of practice to shear a sheep. I was given the task of marking them. Emyr brought me a pail of the semi-liquid pigment, the iron stamp with his father's initials, and showed me the way to use it. Nothing could have been simpler; he wetted the iron, pressed it to the side of the bound sheep, and it was done: the only complication was that sheep of a certain category (they were already marked with a splash of metallic pink on their rumps) were to be stamped on their right sides, and the others on the left.

The sequence of operations did not vary: Emyr or his father would take a sheep from the pen and carry it to one of the fifteen shearers who sat in a semi-circle astraddle on long benches; the shearer, embracing the sheep as it lay half on his lap, half on its back on the bench, would tie its struggling feet with a long thin band of cloth: from that moment the animal would lie motionless and unresisting while the man sheared all the wool from its body: a few minutes, and the fleece, a coherent rug of wool, gray outside and white within, rolled down to the ground at the side of the bench. A woman would pick it up and roll it into a tight ball, and it was my duty to take the sheep, carry it by the feet to the place in the middle where I had my pail and stamp, search it for cuts (I had a black oil for wounds), stamp it on the right or the left, and release its feet.

After a few minutes, while the first batch of sheep were being shorn, I was plunged into unceasing activity. Six or seven sheep came simultaneously from the hands of the quickest shearers; I had to disembarrass their benches at once, so I had a row of sheep lying in the middle. Emyr, as he saw me staggering with a big wether, asked me anxiously if I could manage it. I had never been so close to a sheep before, and its smell and warmth repelled me, and the give of its paunch against my body and the feel of the bones of its legs under their thin shifting skin as I lifted it. I might have cried off in other circumstances, but Bronwen was there in the yard, somewhere behind me. The women of the house were well ahead with their cooking and they had already come out to see the shearers and to roll a few fleeces.

I worked with hard, close concentration. Sometimes an awkward knot on a sheep's feet would delay me, and the sheep would pile up at the benches. Once or twice a sheep, newly released and kicking for its foothold, knocked my bucket over—they often kicked and I had some painful blows from them. Sometimes I could not quickly determine which was the right or the left side of the animal—it is not so easy, with the sheep lying with their heads in every direction: once I untied a sheep before I had marked it, and it had to be caught again. There was the continual necessity of watching the benches, trying to keep pace so that there should be no pile of sheep in the middle. Some boys came. They helped to distribute the *llinens*, the cloth bands the shearers needed for each sheep, and they brought a few of the sheep that were ready to the middle. They were sickeningly brutal to the poor beasts; it was their manliness, and nobody minded.

The sun crept higher and the wind dropped; the noise of the penned sheep was so continuous that I hardly heard it any more, any more than I smelled the all-pervading reek or tasted the dust that came into my throat each time I bent over a sheep—and I bent twice to each, once to pick it up from the bench or the side of the bench, and once to put it down.

Now and then Emyr would come to suggest that I should stamp the sheep more evenly, or higher, and on these occasions, or when I called him to doctor a bad cut, he would do my work with great speed and I would draw ahead of the shearers. Sometimes then for a few minutes I had time to straighten my back and blow some of the stench and dust out of my nose and throat. The group of meager, white, shorn ewes was growing: they wandered wretchedly in the outer yard, calling their lambs. They looked like stunted camels. The initials I had stamped on them stared out on the white, often askew.

Each pause ended with a rush of bound sheep piling up in the middle. Halfway through the morning the pace grew worse, because of the arrival of some shearers who had been delayed. The cries of *Cneu*—a fleece and a sheep ready—and *Llinen* became almost continuous: any small accident, a bad knot, the mark growing too thick, the stamp getting clogged with wool, anything like this threw me behind and submerged me. I had never known that men could work so hard. There was no sense of time any more: it was lifting sheep, sheep and still sheep, the awful belly-strain of it and the tottering walk under the weight to the middle. I had long ceased wondering when they would stop and whether I could keep it up, when the end came. Suddenly there were no more sheep on the benches, only a row of them in the middle, and the shearers were getting up, stretching their legs and straddling about.

I finished and sat down for a moment out of sight by the well with my head between my knees.

Emyr was looking for me to bring me in to dinner. I washed and went with him. The great kitchen was full: long tables end to end with a cloth the length of them and close rows of men down each side. Nain and Bronwen were handing full plates to the men, standing behind the rows. I sat down with Emyr and we began. No one talked. The young men, shy and awkward, whispered and guffawed for a moment and then everybody was eating. They ate fast, with knife and fork together, bent low to the table; the plates were empty and refilled. In ten minutes they had eaten a sheep. Then it was pudding, three sorts of pudding on the plate: slower now, and with a few scraps of talk, but still very fast.

The clatter of spoons died: each man as he finished pushed away his plate. They got slowly to their feet and walked out.

I had done my best to keep pace with them: I was clogged with food, but still I was behind. Bronwen gave me a cup of tea. She said they would be sharpening their shears, and that they would not be ready for a few minutes. I thought she looked at me doubtfully. I had no conversation.

It was a very good cup of tea: I drank it boiling hot and it did a great deal to settle me inside. When I walked out to the shearing place I no longer felt that it was quite impossible to go on. There was a continual shish-shish as they sharpened their shears with little gray hones: some were smoking. They all looked quite fresh.

The afternoon was a repetition of the morning: the sun was hotter and there was even more dust. After some time the women came out, and now I was glad that I had grown a little more adept. The rolled fleeces piled up on the big stack-cover in the middle, and children played in the mountain of wool, jumping into it as they do into hay, and screaming; I was never very fond of children of that age, and now their din irritated me to distraction. From time to time the old man would gather the corners of the sheet and walk off with the wool. The load was much bigger than myself and it looked like those allegorical burdens in pictures. At first I counted them, but as I grew more and more tired I had no attention for anything but the work under my hands. The little boy Gerallt took to pestering me: he wanted to physic the sheep. He took a beastly delight in the wounds that the shearers made, pink triangular flap, and once a ewe's teat shorn clean off. Gentle words had no effect on him, and I was wondering whether I could give him an unseen slap when Bronwen took him away.

Exhaustion came sooner this time. The session went on, went on until it had lasted longer than the morning, and now the shearers were working with surly concentration: they leaned back and rested as each sheep was done—before they had talked and joked, a sound of voices above the noise of the sheep and the snip-snip-snip of the shears.

On and on: sheep and more sheep. I had been doing this forever. My stomach and my back were giving me a great deal of pain, the first from the pounds of food I had stuffed into it, the second from the bend and lift, bend and lift that had been going on the length of this unending day.

I was closed up entirely in the attempt to keep pace, to keep going at all, and I remained like that for a great space of time. If I relaxed at all I would never start again. The inner spur was obstinate anger, nothing more now. It was no longer important that Bronwen was there, picking up the stray pieces of wool into her apron; all that mattered was to keep going, to lift the sheep, mark and release them, and that was everything in life.

It ended, of course: the sun was reaching down to Penmawr and the end came with a trickle of lambs—they had only their tails trimmed and their ears nicked. I was still laboring and closed in over my work when I saw the shearers beginning to get up. I thought it was only the break for tea, but I looked, and the far pen was empty. At the very end were the rams hidden in a pen by themselves: they were taken by the best shearers. I did not think I could lift them, but their horns were a handle, and somehow, lumping them along with my knees I carried them one by one to the middle. With the last ram I could hardly get up after I had marked him: I released him, watched him go, and stayed there on my knees. I thought I was going to be sick.

Some of the shearers were going home, others stayed to help with the driving of the sheep up into the mountain again. I cleaned the stamp, corked the black oil and went away: they called after me to come in for tea, but I affected not to hear.

In my deep chair I tried to relax, but I was twitching all over. In the end I went to sleep there, unwashed and in my filthy clothes, until one in the morning, when I jerked myself awake and crawled off to bed, cold and trembling.

I was very poorly the next day, and for some days after that. Apart from a back as stiff as a board and blistered hands—normal consequences—my old illness began again: it was not very bad, but enough to make me feel rather ill all day and to stop me sleeping at night. Something was wrong with my digestion, as I have said before, and whatever it was (doctors were vague and contradictory) it was linked in some way with my nervous system, and, whenever the one went wrong, the other betrayed me.

There is nothing more contemptible and selfish than a hypochondriac, and I always tried to avoid paying too much attention to my body; but for a man living alone, with a body that will force itself into notice, it is difficult to maintain a sense of proportion.

I did hope for one good from this physical exhaustion and

ill health: I hoped that I should plunge again into my usual habit of mind, and that I should shake off the strong passion that hurt me so. For a day or two it seemed that this might be the case, and I decided to go up to London for a time as soon as I felt better.

But I was deceived. The first day that I did feel equal to a walk—the evening of Thursday—I went down from my garden to the bottom of the valley, across the huge flat slates that made the bridge and up to the Craig y Nos. This is the black precipice that breaks the side of the Saeth ridge, a sudden plunge of harsh granite among the slate and shale: above it there is an apron of green, close grass with an edge of bilberries and fern. It made a charming afternoon or evening walk—it kept the sun late—and I often went up there for half an hour or so in the last of the day.

That evening the sun was hot on the stones and as I sat leaning on my knees, looking forward, I saw Bronwen come out of the farmyard and along to the big ash trees where the washing blew: I could tell her at once by the way she walked. She was wearing a blue dress and there on the brilliant grass under the ash trees she arranged and folded the bellying white sails of the sheets. As soon as I saw her I knew it was no good resisting, and I watched her with what I can only describe as concentrated love. I mean the high-flown term literally: I sent my love across through the clean air down.

At the far end of the road by the cow house, I saw Emyr coming toward the farm. He was coming with his usual steady rapid lurching stride and his road would bring him past the ash trees. She had nearly finished the sheets and I prayed that she would be done and in before he came by. Impatiently I saw her dawdling with the smaller clothes. It would all be spoiled if she did not hurry; she dropped her pegs. He came steadily on, lumbering under my black hate (I managed it then, with no effort) and she was still picking up clothes-pegs from the grass. I willed her, tensing myself inside as I used to do when I was a child, but she would be no quicker: they were both in the same field of vision now—I did not have to shift my gaze to see him level with the first tree. He stopped to do something to the gate, where it was cobbled with string and wire, and she took her basket up and went into the house. It was a strange relaxation inside me; but then he stopped kicking the gate-post and went on. He opened the door with the push of the master, and I followed him in there alone with Bronwen. Even now I am ashamed to set down what a hot, uncontrolled imagination will do.

When the crisis was over I felt the pain. They are right to say it breaks your heart: it is there, just there, you feel the empty, tearing pain, an actual present *pain*, nothing that is going on inside your head, but a great breaking pain, so that you bow over it and cry, with your throat stiff and the sobs coming up from your belly.

I never let it go like that again, not just like that again, so cruel; but once the pain had found its place it did not leave me and it would come there, even when my mind was cold and it had no right to hurt me.

Pugh
====

Emyr Vaughan occupied my thoughts nearly as much as Bronwen. I could not in honesty dislike him. I looked for his faults and they were there, grossness and some ugly ways; and he was, if not downright avaricious, at least very near to it. Once I did see a fox that he had poisoned: it was strychnine they used, and the beast's twisted agony was shocking, even to him. I suggested that he should use something less savage, like cyanide of potassium. He quite agreed that the torture was excessive, even for a fox (he really meant it, for in his way he was humane) but as an unanswerable objection he said, "But, Mr. Pugh, it is costing." They were given the strychnine for nothing. I could see, from the look on his face, that he would do nothing about it—an ugly, shrewd look—so in the end I gave him some cyanide and he threw his old fox-bottle into the fire. But the meanness, if it was true meanness, and the other flaws I saw in him, all came from his way of life and his different values, and they were so far outbalanced by his goodness that they were not ground enough for dislike, still less for hatred.

He was very kind to me: there were continual unprompted neighborly actions, loads of manure when I started gardening, a sack of potatoes, the boy sent up to tell me when anything interesting was going to be done at the farm. He never wanted to be thanked: it was the same when he answered my questions about the working of a farm, questions that must have been childish to a man brought up on the land; he answered them clearly, as plainly as he could, with no mystification or affectation of superiority (there are not so many, in any position, who can do that). He took great trouble in making things clear to me, and when it was a question of manual demonstration, raking or scything for example, he was the best teacher in the world: that was one of the reasons why the farm was so popular among the villagers who wanted their sons to start farming. He was acknowledged as a master in the complex skills of a farmer: I remember a man as far off as Llechog pointing out a stack and saying that it was as well thatched as if Emyr Vaughan, Gelli, had done it.

He had many of the qualities that I lacked—qualities I had always envied in others. He was a great big fellow, to begin with; and he was young. In a way he was good-looking: tall, rather bony, obviously very strong, with red hair and light blue eyes. He had the poor skin that goes with that hair, however, and his eye-lashes did not show at all, which made one think of albinos. Then again, both he and his father had a poor carriage, a heavy and shambling walk, fast enough, but laborious and ungainly; so many country men have that walk, and the same uneasy stance.

On the other hand, he could look downright magnificent. He had brought me up a load of dung one day, a heavy load, and he put the strong young mare to the cart to bring it up. She was turning to vice, nervous and untrustworthy, a huge beast, tight in her skin with muscle, but as quick as a pony.

Emyr had dumped the manure and he was standing at the side of the cart leaning against the wall and talking to me as I stood on the road above him. He was about level with the mare's head, but at that moment he was not holding her. We were talking quietly when for no cause she reared and hurled forward: the shaft drove to crush him against the wall and the wheel to smash him. He was up, lithe as a cat, with his shoulders against the wall and his feet on the shaft, and with the force of his body he thrust the cart out and away from him. It passed clear by inches. He was down and at the horse's head, dragging, hanging and jagging at the bit, tearing her head back in an arch. Then he was in front with a hand on each side of her mouth, forcing her back and back until she stood quiet, sweating and trembling. His face was transfigured: his eyes were blazing and there was foam at his mouth. He took the mare straight down the road, leading her fast and brutally; she was quite cowed.

Whenever I thought of him like that it seemed reasonable that he should be married to Bronwen.

Still, I was willing to dislike him, if I could find a cause: it would have clarified the situation. But I could no longer behave with my former naturalness to him, and that reduced our communication very much indeed, so I could not learn more about him.

It was fortunate that the turning year brought the farm much more work; it enabled me to keep away without remark or offense. I did not quite give up my evening visits; I had been there too often to do so. But they were uneasy visits now.

It was at this time that I made a discovery that others make (I suppose) in their adolescence. I had never understood lyric poetry, sonnets, love-verses before; my taste had been for narrative verse, the Canterbury Tales and the Dunciad I liked, epigrams and *vers de société*. I had perhaps admired the technical ability of the other poets, but behind I suspected that they were rather silly. Now how different it was. I cannot give any measure of the difference. But now Troilus called after Criseyde and my heart ached for him: Marvell could write

> *My love is of a birth as rare*
> *As 'tis for object strange and high.*
> *It was begotten by Despair*
> *Upon Impossibility,*

and he wrote for my understanding; I knew what the words stood for now.

I found, too, that I could tell the difference at once between the right poetry and the artificial: there was all the difference in the world, but I had never known it before.

So there was poetry, a consolation; and there was fishing. Perhaps there is bathos in the conjunction, but there was consolation in both.

But all the time, reading or fishing, or in the ordinary small things of every day, I was with my passion. If you have a sudden painful illness or a broken bone there is hardly a moment when you are not aware of it: it is the same with a heart astray. I was not of a romantic temperament, rather cold, lifeless and indifferent before, not inclined to sentiment at all: indeed, I had sometimes reproached myself for my lack of affection for others. It is a repulsive trait, and it usually goes with deep selfishness; but my life had not accustomed me to affection—I had no near relations, and in the common round of my adult life I had rarely met anyone who raised in me a feeling higher than tepid esteem. My boyhood friends had nearly all been killed in the war, and those who remained were scattered: Maturin was a parson in the north, buried in a huge family (his wife disliked me), Annwyl had a chair of philosophy thirteen thousand miles away, and Milsom was a rubber-planter.

But now, night and day, there was this tumult going on inside me. Everything that I thought or read was in relation to her. The only difference was that at some times it was nearer my consciousness than others: but it was with me, always. It was so improbable—inconceivable, almost—that I asked myself whether I was not exaggerating, deluding myself and nourishing the deception: but I was not. The strength was from outside, beyond my control—a strong hand holding a dangling cloth puppet.

So what consolations I had, I took. I read and I fished— writing was out of the question, and I packed away the dreary, unprofitable sheets. These two things made life tolerable on good days. No: it is excessive to speak like that—I passed delightful hours up there, and there was in fact a more vivid pleasure even in that pain (when it was not bitter and surmounting) than in any of the pleasures I had experienced before.

I say "up there" meaning the high lake above Llyn Lliwiog, a remote barren tarn that was my best retreat. To reach this high lake it was necessary to climb to the Diffwys, to go the length of that dark valley and to climb again the height of the rim at its far end: from there it was a gentle walk down to the lake. There was another way around the back of the Saeth, but there were some shaly slopes that I found almost impassable with a rod to take care of, so in spite of my uneasiness in Cwm Erchyll, I threaded it whenever I went up there.

There is no doubt, I suppose, that lake fishing from the shore is a dull thing compared with the delight of a good stream; but this lake had its advantages. To begin with there was its position of unearthly beauty in a dark crater that spilled the overflowing stream down a precipice five hundred feet to Llyn Lliwiog; below that there was a broad, changing valley with a third lake, much larger, a silver river, farms, woods, the winding ribbon of a main road with tiny objects passing on it. And beyond the silent, tall and solemn peaks of Carnedd and y Brenin, and sometimes single clouds swimming between me and them. Oh, it was intensely moving sometimes, and never two days the same, never predictable.

Then there were fish in the lake, big trout and plenty of them. I never caught any, but I saw them often in the evening: sometimes the air would fall motionless about sunset, and there would be no ripples on the water; every rise showed and upon my word I have more than once seen the whole surface pocked with them like a puddle with rain falling into it. On those evenings I have heard fish rising there so large that it startled the silence. It was a great encouragement to go on fishing, and I would cast away with my arm almost dropping off, vainly lashing the water until long after the end of the rise.

I never was, from my boyhood, one of those to whom skill comes easily. The throwing of a stone at a mark was a conscious effort of coordination rather than an instinctive unthinking fling. It was the same with fishing; every cast was the result of drill and theory—an earnest business. It was a solemn amusement, and I preferred to fish in remote places: it quite spoiled my pleasure if other people were near, to watch, to ask whether I had caught anything—they were in the way even a quarter of a mile off.

I was not pleased, therefore, to see a man come over the skyline as I was fishing on the far side: as he came closer I stopped fishing to change my fly, taking my time in the hope that he would go away. But he took up his place on a rock and I was forced to go on; it was no good, my pleasure was gone now. When I had whipped off a fly I gave up. He came round the lake as I was putting my rod away and said that it was not a very good day for fishing. He was a very old man with a kind, wrinkled face and an air of fragile distinction—I met that quite often in Wales, among the really old people.

We talked for some time and I told him who I was and where I came from: he knew all the older people of Cwm Bugail and most of the younger ones he knew by name, although it was a great many years since he had been there. He asked whether it was not Emyr Vaughan who had married the handsome young woman from Cwm Priddlyd; I said

I thought it was, and looked sharply into his gentle old face for meaning, but there was none there. He came from Nant Deiniol, he said, and I wondered how he had managed that long and arduous climb.

One Friday, as I came over the ridge in the afternoon, I saw him again. I did not distinguish him at first, and I was angry to see a person walking on the shore—I felt, by this time, that the lake belonged to me. I minded less when I saw that it was the old man. He appeared to be towing something on a string as he walked slowly at the water's edge: I could not see anything on the ruffled surface, but his attitude reminded me of a child at the Round Pond with a boat.

He stopped dead on seeing me; I was quite near before he looked up, intent as he was upon the water. But when he recognized me his expression changed from closed hostility to a pleasant smile, and he asked me how all the people in Cwm Bugail were. I walked along the bank with him a little way and then he said that if I was going to fish with a rod he supposed that he would not disturb me by going up and down on the opposite shore. He added that he did not think we should either of us catch anything, because it was a very *hard* day.

On the other side, the rocky side, I put up my rod and began to fish. All the time between casts I saw the old man swing in a slow, steady arc up and down the curve of the farther shore, on the end of his string. There was something restful and inevitable about his progress, and when he stopped abruptly in the middle of his beat it caught my attention at once. He was hauling on his string, winding it on a square of wood, and as I watched a flashing silver fish came up out of the water. I put down my rod and walked quickly round the lake. It was a lovely trout, with golden fins and an iridescent play of colors; the old man said that it would weigh a little over a pound. He was quite pleased at having caught it, but no more excited than if he had picked up a sixpence: he did not seem to think it anything out of the way. He told me about some of the fish he had caught, twenty and thirty a day, or on a summer's night when he was young, and he showed me his machine, that now lay on the shore. He said he did not know the English for it, but in Welsh it was called a stwlan. It was a flat piece of wood, about two and a half feet long, eighteen inches deep and perhaps two inches thick—a piece of good solid plank. The bottom of it was heavily weighted with strips of lead, serving as a keel. In the water the lead pulled the board down so that it was almost submerged, floating upright and very deep— only an inch or two of its top edge showed above the surface. There were two holes in the board, with a string looped through them. His towing line was attached to this loop rather nearer the back of the board than the front, so that when he began to tow it the front pointed out at an angle from the shore, and the board, following its nose, pulled farther and farther out as he let the tight string slip. When it had gone far enough he held the string tight and towed the board against its inclination; it was not a very strong pull, but enough to keep the string straight and clear of the bottom. The essence of the thing was the flies that he attached by short lengths of gut, along the whole length of the towing line: all the way out to the middle of the lake he had flies, separated by a yard, working through the water behind the towing string.

I was charmed with the machine, and the old man showed

me how to use it. It did not exceed my capacity, even at that first attempt: there were some refinements that I did not master, but I made it go out to the middle. It was the cunning jerk that moved the loop of string in the holes, thus altering the set of the board, so that one could reverse, that foxed me, and I was obliged to go on always in the same direction. While I walked round the lake with the string the old man fished with my rod. He said it was a pleasure to fish with a gentleman's rod once in a way, but that he would do better with his stwlan. We neither of us caught anything.

In the evening, when we separated, he told me that he left his board hidden—he showed me the place—and that I was welcome to use it whenever I came up. He said that he left it partly because it was heavy to carry, and partly, he said with a significant look, because you did not want everybody to see you with it.

I could not see why not until long afterwards, when I learned that the otter-board is a poacher's instrument, quite illegal, as well as unsporting. For my part I could never see why it was wrong to work one's flies out in the water with one piece of wood rather than another. If the end of fishing was to catch fish, and if the stwlan would do it when a rod would not, I preferred the stwlan. But I lacked the true sportsman's approach: if there had been a boat up there I would willingly have rowed up and down the lake, pulling a little trawl.

Whenever I went up there after that I used to begin with my rod, partly as a gesture toward the convenances and partly to improve my casting, and then I would take the otter-board and tow it round and round the lake.

I never caught anything: but what a pleasant occupation it was. The top of the board would be out there, perhaps a hundred yards away, just perceptible if you knew where to look, there would be the steady, living pull of the line, and the constant possibility of a sudden jerk from one of the big fish I knew to be there. Soon I came to know the shore so well that I could walk round, passing the marshy places and the rocks without thinking. With this sort of fishing there was just enough to do—a continual gentle motion and a steady, half-conscious watchfulness—to make it a perfect accompaniment for thinking. It suited me admirably. Fly-fishing was too anxious and spasmodic, angling was too dull: plain walking without any destination turned my mind in upon itself. Stwlan-fishing, with its faint dash of raffishness, was the thing for me, and many a day I spent up there, walking slowly round and round the lake, holding the string with my hands clasped behind my back and lines of verse turning, following one another in my head, and my mind running on its eternal preoccupation.

If I had seen her in a house, in North Oxford, in familiar, worn surroundings, would it have been the same? Up there I asked myself that, and until I saw her again I sometimes thought that it would not have been. In the deceiving calm of that high lake I could argue that my being was aroused by its new surroundings: it was a specious argument up there, where I was the only man in the world, and the lake and the mountains had stood since the beginning of time.

I had seen mountains and lakes before: in Switzerland I had seen higher mountains and broader lakes, but there I was on passage, I expected mountains and lakes—I had paid for them and I saw them; they did not affect me: I admired them, but they did not affect me. Here I was not a passing stranger in a tourist's country; here I was in some degree part of it, and I know it affected me deeply. My question was whether it was the mountains, the whole newness, that distorted my judgment; whether perhaps it brought out something that had been latent in me, or whether it was disordered fancy.

But at the sight of her, even far across the valley as I came down, these speculations fled away, and I knew that whatever the force of my present circumstances might be, it would have been the same, in any country, or time, or place.

Bronwen

===

Bronwen Vaughan folded her hands and prepared to answer the questions. Her heart was beating, high quick strokes, but her hands lay calm and folded.

Q. Why did you marry Emyr Vaughan?

A. He asked me. (It did not sound pert: it came slowly, after a turning about for a truthful reply.)

Q. But he did not ask you without any encouragement?

A. No. I do not think I wanted him to ask me though. I was in a flutter, and I do not remember very well what I thought then. I did not think much. I had been quarreling with my sister-in-law.

Q. You said yes at once, did you not?

A. Not quite at once. I waited for a moment and looked at him—we had the stable lantern between us, and he looked so longing. It would have given him a terrible hurt, and he had no protection against it. His face was open and doubtful like a child's: you could not say no. And I suppose the idea of getting away from home was underneath my mind.

Q. Was your home very unhappy?

A. Yes. It was very unhappy.

Q. Tell me about it.

A. It was *our* home when we were children: other people came to visit, but it was our home. My father used to tell me how his grandfather had made the first cart that had ever been seen in the valley: he made it in our cartshed and on the rafter over the door he had left some of the nails, which were a treasure for us when we were children. We were both born there, upstairs in the big bed. Then my father and mother died. I had thought all the world of them, and it made me very sad. For a long time it was all gray and I was very lonely in the house. Meurig told me he was courting and although I felt strange about it I told him I was pleased. She was older than him and I wondered how he could see anything in her at all: she frightened me.

It was worse than I had thought when they were married. Meurig was as kind as he could be: some people said he was soft, but he was not that. She had him down at once, poor Meurig, and he did not even know he was unhappy because she told him he was very fortunate to be a married man now.

The first day she called it "my house." She said she did not like old-fashioned houses. She did not like old-fashioned furniture, either. There was the dresser in the kitchen: it had been put there before the front door was moved, in my great-grandfather's time, and they said that it had been made by William Williams, Pandy, the poet. It had a kind of step underneath it where we used to play shop when we were children. Her first quarrel with Meurig was about selling it to a dealer in Llandudno: he stood up to her for a week, but in the end it went, and they had to take it to pieces to get it out of the door. The kitchen never looked the same again, and until I left home I kept trying to put the knives in the drawer that was no longer there, so I remembered it four times a day. But I must say that I was surprised at the money it fetched: Meurig had got over it by the time the money came, and he was very pleased. He always thought of money the same as sheep. I mean if he had fifty pounds and ewes were five pounds apiece the fifty pounds looked like ten ewes in a pen to him. He loved sheep. I could never blame him when the old things went. He bought some lovely rams, and there were white-painted flimsy things in the place of the old ones.

Q.Was she a bad woman?

A. Oh no.

Q. I mean was she untruthful, dishonest, undutiful, dirty?

A. I suppose she was honest: she was very clean. But she was not dutiful, if that is obeying a good husband in big things. And she was not kind. I think she had a real tenderness for him, but she was impatient with what she called his softness, and she did not think that he could manage as well as she could, ever. I hated her.

Q. Did you not think it wrong to hate her?

A. Yes.

Q.When did Emyr come?

A. We had always known him. His father used to come over for our shearing, although it was far away, and we used to go to theirs. Emyr often came when he was a little boy, and Meurig and he marked the sheep: when he was old enough to shear he always came.

Q. Did you like him as a little boy?

A. Not much. He was always telling Meurig things: he was older than Meurig.

Q. What sort of things?

A. Like a schoolmaster.

*Q.*When did you start to like him?

*A.*Not until a little while before my father's death. It was at the Festival at Dinas, when I had a new dress. It was a very pretty blue spotted dress with a belt that Miss Dashwood gave me—they stayed every summer at the Rectory and they always used to come in and have tea when Mr. Dashwood fished in the lake—it was too small around the waist for her, but it fitted me exactly. I was very pleased with it. It was lovely quality material from London, the best I had ever seen. I did my hair up behind to go with it. At the Festival I saw Emyr staring and staring from the other side, where the young men sit. Any other time he would have come over, but he was too shy now; only when we were going out he came behind in the crowd and talked to Meurig. He was looking at me most of the time and in the end he said, "Well, Bronwen." He did not say anything else until we were getting into the trap, and then I did not hear it, but I was pleased. It had been a very good Festival, better than I had ever heard the singing was; so I had had a fine evening, with my new dress, the singing and being admired, and I liked Emyr for admiring me.

After that he began coming over more often, by himself. At first he hardly spoke to me, but went fishing up in the lake with Meurig. Meurig thought that Emyr came to see him indeed, but I knew better than that. I must have been turned to him a little at that time, because when he came after the Festival I was covered with whitewash from doing the dairy and in my old mac and rubber boots, and I was angry to be seen like that. Before, I would not have minded.

He kept on coming. At the beginning he always had some reason—sheep, or they wanted to buy hay, or did we have a setting of turkey eggs for his mother. Sometimes they were such long-fetched reasons that Meurig stared at him, but my father understood him soon enough, and it came to be that he would come over the mountain once a week without any excuse, on Sunday evenings, usually. It is a very long way by road, and even over the mountains for a shepherd it is better than twenty miles, there and back, but he came, in rain or any weather, and sometimes I used to see him on a good night for the moon, looking up at the house from the river.

Q. Were you in love with him?

A. No. Certainly I was not in love with him: but sometimes when he was not there I thought perhaps I was—little I knew of it, a young girl. I knew that it all gave a kind of new excitement to the days when he came, and I was a long time in front of the looking-glass when I heard his voice below; and I felt a tenderness for him when he sat on the settle bent over with his hands flat between his knees, and nothing to say. He was always shy, and I liked that in a great strong tall man (he was twice Meurig's size). I liked his strength too: he was modest about it, not standing in attitudes or bending the kitchen poker like Griffi Tŷ Hyll. But I knew nothing about him until we were married.

Q. How long were you engaged?

A. Only a little while. Mrs. Meurig wanted me to go, I wanted to be away, and Emyr was impatient: there seemed to be nothing to wait for. Meurig was very pleased: our father had told him that Emyr was a very good young man—he had asked for his character in Pentref long before. Emyr's parents were pleased—I had been over there and they had been to ours, and Mrs. Vaughan had told me that they had been afraid Emyr would never marry—he would never look after any girl but me—and they were very glad he was going to marry such a nice girl. She was such a dear, gentle old lady, and when she sat by me and told me what a good son Emyr was to them, and how they were both old now, I cried.

Q. Was there any arrangement about how you should live?

A. At Gelli?

*Q.*Yes. Were you to come into the house as a daughter?

A. No one said anything about that. I thought about it, but I did not like to say. I supposed it would work out. I know I had no idea of taking the house over from Mrs. Vaughan: I had seen something of that, and I did not want to be anything like Meurig's wife. I thought we would all live together.

Q. What was Meurig's wife's name?

A. Gwladys. Gwladys Evans. Her father was Evans Drapers.

Q. How did she behave at this time?

A. She was pleased about it, and I think she tried to be kind; she would have given me a lot of clothes if I had liked them—shiny satin. She wanted to tell me things before I was married, but I would never let her begin—I said I knew all about it. If it had been anybody else I would have been very glad to have been told.

Q. So you were married.

A. Yes. In church: properly.

Q. Did you go away?

*A.*Yes, we went to Liverpool. We meant to stay a fortnight, but it was miserable, the noise of the trams and the traffic all the time, and crowds; and the English people at the hotel,

Emyr said they were laughing at us. We came back after a week.

Q. Straight to Gelli?

A. Yes.

Q. How did you like that?

A. It was very strange: as strange as Liverpool, only they spoke Welsh. It began badly, because they had not been expecting us, and the house was still upside down. Mrs. Vaughan had been meaning to have it all clean and ready at the end of the fortnight. But they were as kind as could be, and Emyr was very good to me; so I began to settle down.

Q. Will you describe the people of the house?

A. There was the old man, Emyr's father; he was a *good* man. He was true and kind. He was as good as my father, and I liked to be with him. But he had got under the burden of life too young, and he had worked and worked so hard all his life and he had had so much misfortune that it had made him stupid. No; it is wrong to say that of such a good, loving man; but in his old age he could not think of much but work and food (apart from Emyr)—that was all his life except Sundays, when it was chapel. He was a deacon. He was very strict: no one ever smoked or drank or danced at Gelli, and the year's hay would rot if it rained on a Sunday; for no one would think of bringing it in. He did not like stories, or English books from the library. There was not even poetry, and I missed that. It was not that old Mr. Vaughan thought it was exactly wrong, but there was none there, nor music— they none of them had an ear for it nor cared much about it, though they would go to the festivals and eisteddfods. My father had been a lovely poet: he was always competing, and sometimes he won. I thought he was much better than the others I ever heard. Meurig too; but he liked the new way, while my father would never have anything to do with any poems but cynghanedd.

Noson lawen we used to have often in my home: songs and poems—not only hymns, but old songs about things and love. How I missed them; and the piano. I played it, not properly, but enough for the tunes.

Mr. Vaughan was strict, but he was strict without being nasty, if you can imagine that. He was straight through and through, and even Mr. Lewis, Cletwr, the other deacon, could never find anything worse to say of him than that he was selfish and wanted everything in the valley for Emyr. I hardly ever heard old Mr. Vaughan say anything unkind about anyone, except when Mr. Lewis, Cletwr, took Dolforgan (they had three farms already): then he said that they wanted the whole county, and that it was wrong of a rich farmer to take up little farms like that, which should be a living for a family.

Q. What were his faults?

A. While I knew him I never knew him do one thing that he thought wrong. You could say that he worked too hard, so that other people had to too, and that he was mean and selfish. But it was not true: he worked hard because he thought it was right that people should work hard: and as for being mean, he had had such a bad time in the hard years when sheep were worth nothing that he was frightened about money, and guarded it like a weapon—not for himself, but for his family. He *was* selfish for his family, but I am sure he never knew it, and I am sure he would never have done a wrong thing even to have advanced Emyr.

Q. Did he like you?

A. Yes. We always liked one another very much from the beginning. When the others had gone to bed we used to sit together sometimes, and I would read to him, or he would tell me about things that had happened long ago. He loved his food, and I used to cook him the things he liked best. I do not mean that he was greedy, though.

Q. And old Mrs. Vaughan?

A. That was different. I liked her: she was a dear, gentle old lady, and she did her very best to like me at first. But I suppose you can't have two women in a house.

I tried, too, because I liked her and respected her, and I did not want to do anything wrong. I did not go to change anything in the house, and I wanted to take over the heavy work, to rest her. When she was a girl she had worked in the dairy and in the fields, and she had never got into the way of keeping house very well. Everything was shining clean, but it was higgledy-piggledy; and she could not cook. She said she was happier out of doors than in. My mother was a beautiful cook (she had been in very good service) and she always said that I had her hand for pastry: anyway, I enjoyed cooking, and the men liked eating what I cooked.

I brought some of my mother's old things with me—Meurig's wife had nothing to say with them, though she tried—and they looked lovely in Gelli. Before they came the house was rather bare, because the old people had never bought much. Once, when I was not feeling well, I asked Emyr's mother not to paint the cupboard—there was some orange paint over from the cart. She loved painting things: she had mixed the dairy whitewash with sheep-mark for the kitchen, and you could not see anything in the corners of the room, it was so dark. The deep red always came through the next year's coat. When she painted things with real paint they never dried, because she put it on so thick. But I should never have said anything about the oak corner cupboard. It hurt her, and afterwards, when she was not pleased with me, she used to talk about Bronwen's things. "They are in Bronwen's cupboard," or "Look under Bronwen's settle for them."

The real trouble was that she thought Emyr was a god. I should not say that: she thought Emyr was the best man there ever was. She loved him so that anyone who did not think like her seemed to be against Emyr. When Emyr and I quarreled it shocked her, and she thought I must be very wicked.

Q. What did you quarrel about?

A. I could never explain it.

Q. Go on to speak about Emyr.

A. Emyr? Well, Emyr was a good man nearly always. I wondered sometimes that he was so good, the old people made such case of him. He spoke English well; he could read and write it properly, and he was quick at figures. Before, the old man had always had to take his tax papers and all the Ministry forms—there were so many of them—to the schoolmaster, who was very kind, but it meant giving away everything about the farm, which came hard. By the time Emyr was fifteen he could understand them and write the letters, and he could settle with the people at the Grading and write to England for hay and cake and read the instructions on the bottles of medicine for liver-fluke and all the things for the sheep. He was wonderful with sheep, Emyr. The old man was good with cows, but he never really loved the sheep, and he was not fortunate with them; and of course the farm lived on sheep. The milk was just a small thing for spending-money, like the poultry, specially as we often had to buy hay in the winter, because of the bad weather. It was the same with Mrs. Vaughan and the hens: she did her best, but she was never lucky with them. It was not for want of care or hard work, but something always happened. The rats had the eggs and the chicks, or it was the fox (the foxes were terrible in Cwm Bugail). Or there were too many on the ground and they poisoned it, or half of them were broody—there was always something. The marten-cat killed sixty-four in one night.

Q. But Emyr?

A. Yes; I was coming back to Emyr. They used to tell him how clever he was, and of course he saw what a difference it made when he came to be the one who worked the farm and made improvements. If he had not had a lot of real good-ness they must have spoiled him: Mr. Lloyd the schoolmaster was very good for him and often stopped him when he talked too much like a grandfather, and Emyr took it well from him, though he was touchy as a rule.

Q. Did you and Emyr quarrel much to begin with? It often happens at the beginning of a marriage.

A. No, not at first. I tried so hard *not* to quarrel; I hated hard words and the feeling of crossness. At home we hardly ever quarreled, and I never heard my father and mother say anything unkind to one another. I can remember every one of the times when my father was angry with me, and how it hurt.

No, at first I would not quarrel, and in those days Emyr was so kind that we never wanted to, much.

Q. You did not think Emyr was so fine as his parents did. What was it that made you think that way?

A. I saw his faults, I suppose; and they did not think he had any.

Q. What were they? What could an enemy say truly of him?

A. He did not treat his parents right. That was the thing I saw first. He loved them, of course, but he said what was to be done and he worked them hard. He worked very hard too and they thought it quite natural that they should, but they were old, and I hated to hear him say to his father, "No, this year we will have oats in Cefn Bach," or "You will build up the wall by Hafod if I go to the sale this afternoon, isn't it?" He took the nice jobs, like going to the sales: he did that much better than the old man (he was a far better judge of sheep) but the old man loved to go, and meet his friends and talk. I did not like that: and I had never heard a young man contradict his father before. Then Emyr was mean: he knew it and tried hard to overcome it sometimes, so that he spent more or gave away more than was necessary. But it was the real meanness, not like his father, who had been so frightened by not having money that a pound to him was like twenty to another man (when he started farming there was nothing if you failed, and in a hard year it could really be the workhouse or starvation, and the old ones of those days did starve sometimes). With Emyr it was something different and worse: I could see it in his face, over a sixpence perhaps that the servant thought he should have, or over some little thing broken. His voice would change, and he looked horrible: I was ashamed to see him then.

The other thing was with animals. He was as tender and gentle with them as a woman nearly always; very good with sheep and horses, and he physicked them as carefully as children. And he would stay up all night with a cow to help

her with the calf, and he would sit with a bitch although
there was nothing he could do for her and although he knew
that the next morning he would have twenty miles over the
mountain with the sheep to the wintering. But he was no
good with the sheep dogs: he had not the patience for them,
to form them. In my home we had good dogs, and my father
and Meurig worked them with hardly a sound, far up on the
mountain, almost out of sight. Emyr you could hear shouting and whistling every minute: his dogs did not work well;
they would bite the sheep, and often Emyr would get outside
himself. Then he would beat the dogs. He did it much too
hard.

Then when the pig was to be killed, or even a chicken, he
would be excited and talkative in the morning—I did not
understand it at first—and he would do it. He did it very well
and cleanly, but he said he did not like doing it, and I know
he did like it.

That was different from the old man, too. The old man
loved the killing of the pig, but it was different. His face was
honest and happy when the blood spouted: Emyr's was not.

But poor Emyr: he *knew* that there was something, and he
worked against it. It was the same about when he was mean;
he knew that he should give with a good heart, but there was
this thing inside him, and even if he did beat it, the giving
was no satisfaction to him—money, not things; he would
give things. It was the same when he ought to say thank you.
He could not bring himself to it, but you could see him
working to try to bring it out. He would pay a kindness back,
five times over perhaps, but he would not say thank you at
the time.

Q. Was it those things you quarreled about?

A. No: not them.

Q. Did you ever speak to him about them?

A. Only one thing I told him about: I told him straight and plain that if he contradicted his father again with other men there he would do wrong. The other things I could not talk about, except to joke a little about him being near with the money.

Q. What did you quarrel about, then?

A. It was in two ways. At first it was before Gerallt was born. Emyr was a big, strong man: he had a great deal of blood, his mother said. It was winter, and there was not much work to do on the farm—rain and rain all day. I could not—we quarreled then.

He was angry against me and against himself and everything in the world. That was how we quarreled first; but that was not the real thing.

It was after Gerallt was born and I was well again. He had been queer and cross for a day or two, and it was the day of the sale at Llan when the man was gored in the market. He came home excited and queer, and that was the first time he was like *that* with me. Every other time it was when he had done something mean, or when he had been beating one of the dogs. He knew it was evil: he would not speak in the evening, and he would never look at me when he put out the light. He hurt me so.

I hated him then. Hated and dreaded him. I cried and cried: I hated him. He would be so gentle and kind, and so ashamed and he would try to make it right with me; but I hated him.

His mother never knew, of course. Of course she never knew; but she saw me hating him and afraid of him, and then she hated me too, for his sake, although she was so gentle.

We never spoke of it, Emyr and I. We could not. Between times (and it was long between times) we might be friendly together—he would be loving. But I would see his face, and it would be no good.

I behaved badly then. I could have helped Emyr perhaps; but I was afraid of him.

There was something that made it worse. Gerallt slept in our room and the servant on the big landing. I could not cry out and it was quite dark—he drew the curtains tight together. He was terribly strong, I cried all day then sometimes, when I could get away into the hayloft. Once I escaped when I saw it in his face; I lay all night on the mountain, in the fern above Hir Gardd. He came for me before the light and called to me and swore he would not touch me ever, and brought me back, and he was crying. Poor fellow: he could not help it. It was a devil.

But I hated him. I seemed to be alone with him in that house, and no one in the whole valley I could turn to.

Q. Was it often like that again, after?

A. It was again, but it was long, long between and I could almost forget it, it was so long; except in the back of my mind it was always there, and even when we were kind and friendly somehow I was half-watching him.

Q. Go back to the old people. What did Emyr's father think?

A. He never knew anything about it at all. If I cried he thought it was just a woman crying—a headache, something—and he would talk soft and tread quietly, but he never knew anything. Nain—we began to call the old ones

Nain and Taid after Gerallt was born—Nain must have told him how bad I was, but he was always kind to me.

Q. And old Mrs. Vaughan?

A. It went against her nature to hate me, and she was so good in all her other ways that once I almost told her. But once she had seen me hating her son, not bearing to touch him or even give him a word (I could not help it; I felt like a wild animal the next day) she turned against me with all her might. She would not have stopped to kill a man who threatened her son, I know.

Of course she had been jealous from the beginning: she said it herself—laughing at first and said I must not mind because she would get better. But now, with poor Emyr trying to make it right (he meant every time never to do it again) and me flouting him so cruel, the old jealousy swelled up. I was afraid to show him any countenance: I did not want to, but I thought I ought to be even harder than I felt, to try and master him. She suffered for him, and she could not rest. Nothing I could do was right—it was her trying to attack me for him—and she would speak to me sharply all day long until at last Emyr flew out at her. I think it made his conscience even worse, seeing me used so, and he was very hard to her that day. Then she was different. She *would* do the hard work; she would not be helped, though it made my heart bleed to see her: she would say, "Bronwen says it should be like this," or "Bronwen wants me to do that." And it was "Bronwen's settle" and "Bronwen's sheets" always now, until I wished Meurig's wife had had them all: and she spoke of their things as separate, to make me a stranger.

I tried to keep things looking ordinary: I would have put my hand in the fire rather than spoil the old man's home.

There was one more thing. After Gerallt was born and before Emyr began to be like that, I was happy for a long time. My dear brother often came over to see him—I used to tell him he would not come to see me, but he would let the sheep look after themselves all day to see Gerallt. He promised me Gerallt should have our old home, because the doctors had said that Gwladys could not have a baby, and it made me wonderfully happy to think of my son in Cwm Priddlyd.

Emyr was very kind to me then; he was so pleased with Gerallt. Gerallt was a lovely baby: no woman could have wanted a better one. Emyr brought me a lot of books about children, and we read them. Nain and Taid loved Gerallt, but they did not think anything of the books.

The old ones were very bad when Gerallt stopped being a baby. Taid wanted him to have everything that he wanted, at once. If ever I had to correct him (and I know I was very weak in correcting him) it was as if I was a dragon. Taid said, "Never put a hurt on a child," and he looked at me more gravely than he ever had before. And Nain said, "This is the way I brought up Emyr."

More and more Emyr would go over to their side and kiss and hug Gerallt when he was roaring: but I would *not* give up my child to them. Whenever they had Gerallt to themselves they would put a month's spoiling into an afternoon, and I saw him turning into a bad-mannered, ill-natured little boy before my eyes. What was so very, very much worse was that I thought I saw him being cruel, in a sly way, like Emyr was in his times. This was after the great trouble, and when he had been going about by himself for a long time in the yard and far into the fields. I would *not* give him up.

But what can you do when three grown-ups side with a child against you? If you are strict he turns from you; if you are not, you are not doing what is right. It nearly broke my heart, sometimes. I did so want him to grow like my father or Meurig, and they were making him a child I was ashamed of, apart from that thing that I feared. He was such a beautiful little boy, that was part of the trouble: even the doctor said he had never seen such a well-made, healthy child.

It made me angry every day, and in the end I found myself talking with a voice like Meurig's wife. I suppose I should have managed it better. I was always sorry after I had put him to bed; but the next day it would be the same, and I would hear Nain say, "There. But don't tell Mam." Or he would do some little wrong thing and run from me to Taid or his father.

Q. You have not spoken about the servant.

A. We had several. They used to come when they left school and when they were sixteen they would go, because they had to be paid much more. Their parents used to like them to start at Gelli, because they knew they could not get into mischief with old Mr. Vaughan there, and they would learn to work well. The boys used to complain about the food and say they were worked too hard. They were worked hard, very hard, for growing boys, but I saw they were well fed when I cooked for them. They were good boys, most of them; Tudor Taiduon and Bleddyn from down in Llan were very good boys indeed, although Bleddyn got into trouble after he left us. The only one I did not like was Siencyn Griffiths, a nasty boy; but they all said he was very good at school and in chapel. He did not like farming, and in the end he went to train for a schoolteacher. They said Mr. Lloyd yr Ysgol paid for his training; he was always very good to his boys, and he helped several of them with their training, or things like that. Then of course there was Llew at the end, after John.

Q. Did you know Mr. Lloyd well?

A. Not very well.

Q. He had a great influence on Emyr?

A. Yes, I am sure he did.

Q. What sort of man was he?

A. I always heard good of him. It was a great thing for the village to have such a good teacher there. He was often offered to be headmaster in bigger places, with men under him and a better house and more money, but he stayed. He was very good to his boys: they all said that, the boys themselves; and a boy with Mr. Lloyd's good word could get a place anywhere in Llanfair or Dinas, and he sent a lot on to the County School.

Q. But you did not like him?

A. I respected him very much. Everyone respected Mr. Lloyd.

Q. Did you dislike him?

A. No. I did not dislike him.

Q. You have said a lot of good things for him: what could be said against him?

A. Nothing really against him. Perhaps he liked to rule. People said that he liked everything his way. Well of course he was the best-educated man in the valley, so he knew what was best: even if he did not, he always gave a good example and helped anyone who was in trouble.

Q. Did you ever think of speaking to him about Emyr? He had known him all his life, and he had taught him. You could have spoken in a very round-about way.

A. Oh no. No; that would have been quite impossible. Even if I had thought of it, I know that he would not have been wise enough. He was very good and well-educated, but he was not a wise, deep man.

Q. Did he come often?

A. At first he did, fairly often, but less after a while. I was afraid he did not like me, although I always made him very welcome.

Q. You did not like him, of course?

A. No.

Q. Now—you know I am not here to praise or blame— that I am only here to ask for the truth: it is my duty. I do not want to hurt you at all. You know I must ask you—(in the pause she waited, silent: she knew that he was giving her time to gather fortitude. Her heart broke quietly again, but when he went on she was ready to answer; only her hands were clasped tight now)—we must talk about Mr. Pugh.

Pugh

I must go back a little in the order of time and break my narrative to describe my acquaintance with Skinner. When I took Hafod I had understood that there were practically no gentlefolk within calling distance, and this seemed to me in many ways an advantage. Perhaps, having rubbed shoulders for so long with more people than I liked, I saw it as a disproportionate benefit; but with all allowances there is something to be said for the absence of formal, enforced intercourse. One may be lucky and chance upon a set of amiable neighbors, liberal and informed, who can make life much more pleasant. It is more probable that no such thing will occur, and that one will be condemned to a round of tea-parties with neighbors whose only point of contact is speaking the same dialect. It is so easy to become involved in local jealousies, and to be obliged to go on seeing acquaintances whom one cannot drop because it would be wounding and incorrect.

Here the local landowner lived in a house out of reach when he visited Wales (which was seldom), and his agent lived at the far end of the estate, ten miles beyond the Plâs. The parson was what might be termed a career-clergyman. He was a collier from the south who had shown a good deal of scholastic promise in his boyhood: this had opened many possibilities to him, and casting about for a life that would assure him security, ease and prestige he had fastened upon the Church. I do not know how livings are arranged in the Church in Wales, but however it was, he had appeared in this parish some twenty years before, and by all accounts (I am repeating vulgar, ill-natured gossip) he had instantly given up all further ambition. When he came there had been a congregation sufficiently numerous to fill the old church on great days. Now two old ladies resentfully listened to him mumbling through the obligatory duty, and the noncon-formist chapels were fuller than they had ever been.

I went down at Christmas and Easter and sat among the dust and the droppings of the bats. Each time I came away angry and sorry for the old church—it was built in the four-teenth century, and it had one or two fine tombs.

I am afraid he took a malicious pleasure in his nastiness; but he was immovable, so long as he committed no ecclesias-tical offense, and he never did that. He led a strange torpid life in the week, doing nothing in the kitchen of the rectory, in a state of great sordidness. The gardens had been left to grow wild, except for a little square of potatoes half-buried in the wilderness: tall grass had invaded all but the very mid-dle of the gravel drive, and once as I passed I saw a pale, lean sow between the noble magnolias that had survived and the lovely petals were dropping slowly on her back.

I talked to him once or twice. With all my respect for his cloth, I found it difficult to be civil: he had a fawning, obsequious manner that I suppose he had picked up on the principles of Heep in his younger days, but now it was mixed with an intolerable confidence. In the first two minutes he asked half a dozen impertinent questions, and all the time he kept touching either my elbow or my shoulder.

However, by this time I had been a long while without seeing anybody but the people in our valley. It was during a very painful time—I had not grown hardened to it at all—and more than ever I was thrown in upon myself. So I was not altogether sorry to see a man coming up my path one morning between showers. I knew him by sight, having passed him often enough in the lower village and in Llanfair: he was a Mr. Skinner, who lived at Tan yr Onnen—a bachelor.

He came rather furtively up the path, with his hand in the pocket of his coat; he was frowning, and I had the instant impression that he would be very glad to find his knock unanswered so that he could push his note through the letter box and go away.

I gave him a glass of muscat. He was ferociously shy and would do nothing to help the small-talk along. He seemed to dislike me and I wondered why he had come: when he got up to go he said that he hoped I would take tea with him on Thursday. I said that I should be very happy, but when I had closed the garden gate behind him I thought that I should probably send a civil excuse: it was a long way and we appeared to have nothing to say to one another.

By Wednesday I had done nothing about it, so on Thursday I put on a clean shirt and walked down the valley to the main Llanfair road, and along it to the lane that led to Tan yr Onnen. Skinner's house was a dark, severe building: it had been built about eighty years ago, and the whole of its outside was covered with big overlapping purple slates. It was comfortable enough inside, though, and the room in which Skinner received me had a good fire, a Turkey carpet and shining brass fire-irons. There were comfortable chairs and the walls were lined with books. Skinner was much more at his ease in his own house than in mine, and he put himself out to be a good host. We talked about the neighborhood, the weather, and somehow we got onto chess: he asked me if I played. I did, a little, I said—in point of fact I rather piqued myself on my game. Bridge and chess; those and domestic comfort were the only things that I missed. Bridge to a less degree, because it is so rarely possible, even in the best conditions, to gather four civil players of equal skill at one time, and bridge under any other conditions is a torment. He proposed a game after tea, and I was very glad that I had said I was out of practice, as well as being an indifferent player, because he beat me twice running with humiliating ease.

When I went home, much later than I had expected on setting out, I was pleased with my afternoon and I looked forward to seeing Skinner again.

He was a difficult man to know well. We had exchanged several visits before I knew anything about him at all. He was very reserved, and in this case I could not gather information about him by asking my neighbors. They knew that we were acquainted, but they offered no remarks. I do not know that I liked him very much. He was so hedged in by his shyness and a long habit of withdrawal that we remained at a distance for a long time. He was remarkably ugly, too, and it is difficult to overcome a prejudice against ugliness. When we did grow more confidential I did not care much more for him: he was intelligent in a way—thought for himself—but there was something hard, sterile and selfish down there, and it appeared to me that he did not have nearly enough ballast of solid information for his solitary thinking to be of any value. With all his diffidence he had a pretty high conceit of his intellectual abilities: I do not think that he had often mixed with men better informed than himself.

His superiority in chess supported his opinion, and I must say that he played a good game. I tried very hard indeed to beat him and occasionally I succeeded, but he was really outside my class. He had a wide theoretical knowledge (which I lacked) so he had to work much less with his head than I did; the result was that my concentration would fail toward the end, while he was still thinking as clearly as at the beginning; I would make some foolish error and it would all be over—I could never afford to make a slip with him. He favored a very closed queen's pawn opening and an involved, complex middle game. This had something in common with his character; but while his thinking worked out well in chess, where the logical connection is predetermined, in more important things it did not.

However, he enabled me to pass many hours that would have been hard to bear otherwise. We nearly always played chess, but sometimes it would happen that I was out of form (a heart wrenched sideways, that was the real trouble) and I could hardly give him a game; when it was like that and I had been beaten three times in a row, we would sit and talk.

Skinner had been a magistrate until a few years before: I gathered that he had retired, or had been asked to retire, because he declined to administer some law or regulation that he considered unjust. He did not go into it, supposing me, I think, to be au courant, but I believe he had made some very strong remarks from the bench. I could well imagine it; he had a fund of nervous violence that almost got the better of him at times, when we spoke of some controversial subject. His time as a justice of the peace had given him a particular insight into the life of the people, and he had many interesting things to say about them. It had also distorted his view. I was surprised to see how little allowance he made for this distortion: he saw the local inhabitants as a bitterly litigious quarrelsome, perjured crew, drunkards, bloody and revengeful. He also attached much too much importance to those crimes like incest and bestiality and to bastardy cases—they are common enough, but they do not appear in the papers, and they had taken him by surprise and shocked him very much. He had led a curiously pure life; he was a natural bachelor, and perhaps there was some abnormality there.

I suppose he liked Wales. He lived there voluntarily: there was nothing to detain him if he did not like the country. Yet I cannot call to mind any occasion on which he said anything pleasant about the inhabitants: dozens of his stories occur to me; they all showed the Welsh in a bad light.

One of the things that he held against them as a particular national vice was their admiration for Englishmen. "There is this stupid provincial chauvinism on the one hand," he said, "with all the fandango about the language and nationalism and so on, and on the other hand a servile imitation of Liverpool manners. Once they get on a bit, what language do they talk? English every time, unless they want to make political capital out of Welsh. When there was an English regiment stationed here alongside a Welsh one, who did the girls go with? The Englishmen, always. Where's the Welsh gentry? It is either extinct or anglicized. Anyhow, the mob does not look up to it—the spirit is too mean for respect—the summit of their social ambition is to be a doctor, a minister, a chemist or a teacher. It is a society where the lower middle class is the top, like in America. There's nothing generous or open about it.

"The values they respect are false; good manners and social distinction must be imported to be any use. Where can a mediocre, rather vulgar Englishman settle and become a local bigwig simply because of his nationality? Only in Wales.

"No, no; there is no real national pride: nothing deep and steady, no self-respect, only hysterical play-acting. They affect to despise England and the English, but they prostitute their country to char-à-bancs full of the scum of Lancashire and Stafford, and when an Englishman of some means settles among them, they lick his boots."

I ventured to question a great deal of what he said, but he had grown excited—he was walking up and down, biting his nails, and I saw, that apart from registering my disagreement, there was nothing I could usefully say.

"Oh, I know very well that you do not see it as I do," he said, "but believe me, I have been here a good many years, and I started out thinking as you do. I found them very sympathetic: I found their respect very flattering, and being half Welsh on my mother's side I thought I was more or less one of them. I began learning their language, and I deluded myself that I would thoroughly understand them and identify myself with them in a year or two. But the more you know about them the less you like them, and anyhow you never come to the point where you think as they do. You may suppose them to be open, simple people—the mountain farmers, at any rate. But they are not. They just make a fool of you. They are a closed race, and you never arrive at understanding the motives that lie behind their actions. You see the results, and you condemn them; but you cannot see farther than that. It was, in fact, one of the farms near your place that gave me my first insight into their character—one of the nicest farms you can imagine."

I asked him whether in this day and age it was really worth talking about national character: I was trying to turn the conversation, because I did not like him when he talked in this enthusiastic, overwrought way.

"No, not in most cases; but in the case of the Welsh, yes; certainly. You must have noticed how strongly their national types are marked. There is the little dark lard-faced kind you see in draper's shops and dairies all over England and in the Welsh towns. Then there is the bony-faced sort with high cheekbones and widely separated eyes and a nose with hardly any bridge—gray eyes, usually, and medium height. And then there is the tall sandy-haired lean type—the ancient Britons, as I call them: they are exactly what that Roman (Suetonius or Agricola, which is it?) described, and they have stayed the same. Take the children in the village, there is never any doubt for a moment who they belong to; they all look exactly like their fathers or their mothers. They always breed true. You can cross them how you like, but the children always come out little Welshmen, with the same mental reactions—you may shake your head, Pugh, but it is the case [I was thinking, in point of fact, of himself as a living contradiction of what he said] and you will come round to my way of thinking if you stay here long enough. No, the blood is as strong as Jewish blood, and the Welsh parent is always the dominant partner from the genetic point of view. [What the devil have you or I to do with genetics? I thought. It is an exact science.] That is why I feel justified in talking of a national character. But I will tell you about these people at the farm.

"I do not think I would be breaking any rules if I were to tell it with names and places—it was nearly all out in public at the end—but perhaps I ought to change the names and ask you not to repeat the details.

"These two brothers, and the wife of the elder, farmed . . . well, Tŷ Bach. The younger was a widower, childless, like the others: he was a more retiring, timid man than his brother, and something of a bard. It was an ideal ménage. They were not well off, but they were comfortable; that corner of land is fertile, and although it is small it kept the three of them even in bad years. They had an excellent understanding among themselves and they worked together like characters in a moral story-book. I speak of what I know, because the younger one gave me Welsh lessons, and I saw them at all times. They would not have been anything like so comfortable with children—apart from the expense the house was very small. It was a long house: there are still a few of them inhabited, you know—those long low old houses with the people on one side of the passage and the cattle on the other, with one big kitchen and a half-loft over it and

hardly anything else. The dairy was part of the main room—
an alcove behind the chimney-breast—and hens were walking in and out all the time. It was the kind of room where a
wireless set looks mad, like something out of another world.
I don't know how people ever manage to bring up children
in those places, but they do: I knew a family of thirteen in
one.

"However, there were no children in this case. A little
farther down there was a widow with five or six. She was said
to be a widow, but I don't know that anybody had ever married her. She was one of those curious things, a rural
whore—well, perhaps not whore, because I doubt if she was
ever paid, but the children all had different fathers. She was
a hideous slattern, mentally deficient I think, and apparently
quite old, but still year after year she produced these children.

"I must say this for the people up there, that although
they would not have anything much to do with the woman
they were kind to the children. They went to the village
school with the others, the schoolmaster saw to it that there
was no difference made, and there were people who gave
them proper clothes and taught them cleanliness and took
them into their homes.

"The people I am talking about, the Evanses, had a particular fancy for the second boy, who was called Alfred—his
father was probably an English vagrant. Alfred was always at
Tŷ Bach, a well-mannered little chap for a Welsh boy—not
that that is saying much, because they are the most indulged, spoilt set of brats I have ever come across—and he
helped with all the things that a boy can do. I used to see him
eating enormous meals there at all hours of the day, and it

was some time before I understood that he was not of the household.

"Well, as I was saying, these people pretty well made themselves the foster-parents of this lad. I could bring dozens of instances as evidence of mutual affection, encouragement, and so on and so forth. But the point is that the boy was thoroughly liked by the childless, middleaged people of Tŷ Bach.

"Very well. In the winter the brothers were cutting chaff. You have seen the big external water wheels in most of the farms? This one still worked; they had a good stream, and the wheel churned the milk, cut the chaff and turned a grindstone.

"You cut chaff by feeding straw into the machine at one side: toothed rollers carry it in and a large, heavy wheel with curved blades attached to its spokes cuts it into short lengths. The wheel revolves very rapidly and makes a deafening noise when it is cutting.

"The younger brother was shoveling chaff into the storage place; the elder was in the straw-loft. The boy was feeding straw into the machine: he had been told not to touch it.

"The elder brother heard Alfred scream, but before he could get down from the straw the mischief was done: the younger brother, on the other side of the machine, did not hear the scream but did hear the changed note of the cutter and ran to stop it. He kicked the driving-belt off and between them they got the boy's arm out. The hand was gone just below the wrist and the forearm was terribly mangled: he was bleeding profusely and he was unconscious.

"There was one thing clear in the subsequent confusion: a case for damages could be brought against them. They had not expressly invited the boy; they had even told him not to touch the machine, the guard of which was defective; but the case might lie.

"They carried the boy through the blinding rain to a shaft some three hundred yards from their house. It was an unsuccessful trial shaft for a slate quarry and they used to throw their dead sheep down it instead of burying them in the shallow earth. The boy was certainly unconscious, but whether he was dead or alive when they threw him down was never established. They threw rocks and earth on top of him.

"Very well. There were inquiries made, but they came to nothing and it was supposed that Alfred, who was a forward, adventuring lad of thirteen, had gone off on a lorry to seek his fortune perhaps at sea. He was big for his age, precociously self-reliant, and he was determined to be a sailor in time. There were plenty of long-distance lorries passing on the main road, and once before Alfred had gone as far as Swansea before being discovered.

"In seven years the brothers fell out. The woman was now about forty or forty-five; her personality appeared to change radically and she no longer made the house comfortable for them. She would no longer cook: their meals came out of tins or they cooked them themselves. The atmosphere of the house was poisoned by her nagging.

"What brought their quarreling to a head was the deaconry of the chapel—I mean which should be deacon now that there was a vacancy. The younger brother was the literary one of the family, but the elder had the elder's rights. They had both taught in the Sunday school for many years, though of the two the younger was the more active.

"You know the great importance of the chapels here, and

the prestige and influence a deacon has: you can hardly overestimate it in the high farming valleys where there is no other authority or public opinion—where public opinion is integral and undiluted, I should say.

"God knows what went on up there in Tŷ Bach, but the outcome of it was that when it was certain that the elder brother was going to be the deacon the younger denounced him to the police.

"Well; there you are. Those are the sort of people we have to deal with: you see my point?"

"Yes, I see your point perfectly well, but I do not see how you can argue that the Evanses were typical or that this ghastly affair has any bearing on the national character of the Welsh. After all, on that basis you could go through the Newgate calendars of every country and prove the survivors the greatest rogues unhung."

"Hm. I suppose I have explained it badly. It was not the thing itself that I was meaning, but the manner of it, and the motives."

"Yes, I appreciate that. But I still think that you could duplicate the whole of it elsewhere. Surely you do not intend to confine hypocrisy, violence and self-seeking to the Welsh. I am very sure that they do not have a monopoly; and more than that, I should say, saving your presence, that they have a larger share than usual of the contrary virtues."

I thought he was going to answer angrily, but he checked himself and said, "No. I have not chosen my case well. It does not really bring out what I meant to say—and the rest obscures it. I should have emphasized the *closedness* of these people, the fact that I was on terms of friendship with them—that the boy was—and that I knew nothing about them, never pierced through the barriers to see what sort of people they really were—and this *after* they had done it. That's the important point. I was there within a matter of days of the crime, and I took my tea in a happy, model family and went over a number of englynion that the younger brother had just written."

There were a good many replies that came to my tongue, but I could not say them in his house. He went on eagerly, "You must have come across it. I am sure you will recognize it if you reflect. You know the Thomases at Hendre, don't you? Or even more the people at Gelli—that is the place where the old man and his wife came from Cwm y Glo, isn't it? And where the young one married a girl from Cwm Priddlyd recently? Yes, of course it is. Well, what do you know of the good people at Gelli? You think you know them pretty well, don't you?" He paused and seemed to recollect himself; he looked at me for a moment, and I did not know how to interpret the look: I thought he was going to go on. He hesitated, fiddling with a pawn, and said in a different voice, "It's a matter of years, perhaps. In the end you'll come round to my way of thinking." Then he began to rearrange the chessmen.

Pugh

It was toward the autumn that I began to feel so continuously unwell. I know it is ridiculous to keep harping on this, but I do insist upon it because a man (myself, at any rate) is ruled by his stomach. If it does not behave well one's whole outlook on life is changed, and I really believe one's character changes with it.

My choice of a doctor was not fortunate: Davies had been an Army doctor for a long time and in Dinas he had a very large panel practice. I went to him on a vague recommendation and never after summoned up enough moral courage or energy to change. Changing doctors in the country is a great upheaval, and even if the other man had agreed to it he might have turned out worse. I did not often go to Davies or send for him; I was willing to be impressed, but I had no confidence in his *mist. alb.* or his brisk "No beef or mutton." He would have cut off a leg or set an arm with the best, but he was not the man for me. What I wanted was one of those quiet, humane doctors who have few patients: they sometimes go into semi-retirement in country towns and doctor their friends from kindness and a desire to go on being useful; they do take notice of their patients, and even tend to coddle them. I knew such a one in Thame, and I lost a good friend when he died.

If I had been a good physician to myself, I should have refrained from going down to the farm and from spending my afternoons on the Craig y Nos staring down to see Bronwen. It was always worse after that; but if I did not see her there was such a strong impatience in me, a tearing restlessness, that it had the same effect and I would find myself as nervous as a cat, unequal to my food, useless for reading or settling to any sort of work. As for my book, it had dropped into the utter distance; the pseudo-Basil and the nameless monks whose work I had transcribed into so many heavy notebooks for so many heavy years, and who had occupied my slow thoughts for such a dull length of time, they were as far from me now as I was from my old self.

Nothing seemed worthwhile, and I am afraid that I let the household chores slide day after day until I was living in a slum. And how slowly the time passed. I had a little chiming clock that beat the quarters: as each passed after an empty gray space it seemed that I had gained something; and the hours were a victory, each one. I would not have minded so much if I had been able to sleep.

I felt I was a constraint on them down at the farm, but I still went in the evenings: earlier on, when the surprise—the shock, even—had been new to me, I had almost stopped my visits, but now I went down quite often. I could not keep away and now, more than ever, I wanted to know whether I was right about Bronwen and Nain.

I had noticed it in the first place, at a time when my perceptions were dull—how dull, and what a heavy clod I must have been for all those years of my life; half alive, no more.

Now it was essential for me to know whether I had been right then, when I was an unmoved spectator. All the innumerable little things that had given me that impression seemed to point out that Nain was not being properly used. I had my periods of reaction, when I told myself that I was making a fool of myself, creating an image of Bronwen that had no relation to herself apart from physical resemblance. Then I would be sorry for my treachery, and go all the way back again.

But there was something there, and the more I thought about it, when I was balanced between extremes, the more I felt its importance: because if she was in fact hard and unkind and dispossessing towards Nain, then she was not the woman I was breaking my heart for. I said that that would be for the best: I could go away then. Then I tried to see Emyr's share in it (he was not always kind, and rarely considerate) and I tried to exculpate Bronwen, to lay it all on the difference of habit and tradition, the different way of life. But in the end I wanted the truth. The truth—no comfortable deceit or compromise—that was the essential.

I was afraid of what I might find, and as time went on I became more afraid. It was all very well to say in my mind that I wanted my release; it was a damned lie. I wanted my love made certain, confirmed, redoubled; but my heart was afraid. (I cannot talk of this without the sound of romantic clap-trap: I am sorry for it.) I was very willing to search for the truth if it should tend in the direction I wanted, and I hated the search for it when everything seemed to point away.

But I had to have the truth. They talk about love being blind: I did not want to be blind—for that matter, I do not think I ever wanted to be in love.

I went on and on at this prying, eavesdropping, spying, and I heard many things that hurt me to the quick. Nain, and the others in the farm, spoke of "Bronwen's table, Bronwen's dresser, Bronwen's teapot." It seemed that her *dot* was quite outside the common stock: certainly the things that were called hers were very much better—there was the prettiest little oak gate-leg table that I have ever seen outside a museum: they used to give me my tea on it: "Sit down, Mr. Pugh, sit down: I have putting your tea to Bronwen's table, isn't it."

Always, if I asked Nain anything, she would refer the decision to Bronwen. I remember so clearly walking into the back kitchen, where the old lady was scrubbing on her hands and knees (the scrubbing brush and pail looked too big for her): she looked up and put her hand to a loose wisp of white hair. She said good morning with a smile on her tired, gentle old face and when I asked her whether I might have an extra half-pint of milk she called up the stairs to Bronwen: I did not hear what Bronwen said, but the sound of her voice was not very pleasant, and as I went from the house I heard the little boy Gerallt beginning to cry.

How depressing it was. It was one out of a great many instances—not conclusive (I would have taken a great deal of convincing, but I was sufficiently honest to have accepted a downright proof), not conclusive, but they mounted up, accumulated.

It is usual, I imagine, for a man to look for perfection where he loves: I was rather old for a lover; I was willing to compromise for much less, and if she was curt with Emyr that did not concern me—there might be so many things there that I could not understand, nor possibly judge—but I had to have a nature that would not be unkind to Nain, would not dispossess her of her place in the house where she had been the mistress for thirty or forty years, a nature that could not reduce the old lady to a super-annuated servant.

Perfection was there when we all sat in the farm kitchen, but when I lay in bed thinking it over, piecing my evidence together, playing the *advocatus diaboli*, what a black picture presented itself.

If it really did come down to a commonplace usurpation, dominating usurpation, what could be more wounding? And what other answer could there be? I struggled very hard against the idea (and, with a stupid wrongheadedness, toward it: duty seems so often to lie along the more unpleasant road, and the unacceptable notion is so often the correct one. But I am not to be talking of duty here).

To abridge a little: I worried myself into a pretty state by the autumn. It was a weeping autumn, no St. Martin's summer, no memory of summer but the little sad piles of hay that rotted in the fields, and the brown fern decayed on my place above the Craig y Nos.

I had disagreed with Skinner. I had thought we might in the end, but it had come sooner than I had expected. To my astonishment it turned out that he was one of those people who believe that the English are Israelites: he did not speak about it until we knew one another quite well, but I should have guessed it from his books. I tried to keep him off the subject when it did appear that this was his belief, but he would talk about it, and one day when my heart was excoriated he chose to show me the logical grounds for his belief. I do not know whether he was one of the orthodox school (he thought we were descended from only two of the tribes)—I knew nothing about it except that the belief existed—but with him, he said, it was a matter of reason, not of faith, and he tried to convince me that right was on his side. I should never have entered into the discussion, but I did. The stuff he adduced was such an intolerable farrago of rubbish that I was shocked that it should have imposed upon a man of education and some reading. It was such an incoherent, verbose mumbo-jumbo, with esoteric twaddle jostling gnosticism, scholarship of the *lucus a non lucendo* order that I could not refrain (burning with my private fire) from saying some sharp things about his authors. I should have been quiet; of course I should, if only from civility, but I was not, and we parted on very formal and rigid terms.

I had touched him home once or twice: what he was talking about fell to pieces if you jarred it with a hard fact, and in spite of his taking refuge in a cloud of mystical jargon he was a man of some intelligence, and he must have felt the truth of some of the things that I said. I did not expect him to like me any the better for it, but I was not prepared for the letter he sent up by a boy: it was a violent, unbalanced letter, written in a tearing hurry, and it contained many rude statements of a personal nature, most of them false. Its manner, and some queer inversions, made me wonder whether the man were not off his head. There was nothing to say; no reply to be made. It made me sad for that day, and often afterwards when I remembered Skinner's kindly side and our games of chess.

When you are ill, if nobody with authority tells you that you are particularly unwell, or knocks you down with the name of your disease, it is surprising how long you can go on living an ordinary life. There was Ransome, who broke two ribs falling off a ladder in the Bodleian, and took pneumonia. I saw him looking poorly, and when I asked him he said that he was very indifferent, and that he had a heavy cold: he had no doubt about carrying on with his work. When he was examined, however, and they told him that it was pneumonia and broken bones and put him to bed, he instantly began to speak in a feeble, exhausted whisper, with his eyes half-closed. Far be it from me to make game of Ransome: I do not think that he was malingering at all. I only mention him to show that one can walk about when one is in a really dangerous condition.

This was the case with me: there was a whole week when I dragged myself about, either unaware that I was seriously ill or denying it to myself. By the end of the week I had let everything slide; the cottage was in a horrible mess, but I lacked the courage to start setting it in order: even the effort of getting the milk from the farm was too much at the end—besides, I no longer possessed a milk jug that was not crusted with sour milk. I just sat over the fire and drank pot after pot of weak tea, letting time pass over me, day and night (I remember filling the lamp). Then the fuel ran out, and I crawled up to bed. The stairs were longer and steeper than ever.

Once I heard the postman, and I thought of calling to him, but while I was thinking about it he came and went. I heard the garden gate close behind him: he had a particular way of shutting it, with a sharp clack.

The clock stopped, and with it my own sense of the passing of time. It stopped as it was striking; the strokes went longer and longer, and the last came far behind, somberly.

It was a lethargy, not unpleasant, but gray and toneless. I was right down there, far down, sunk down and very quiet. I was there all right, and perfectly aware of myself, but reduced, very small and quiescent. My body had stopped hurting much. Only if I moved it hurt. I could lie quiet though. All that old griping and tension was gone and it was as if my body had consented to let me lie in peace so long as I did not bother it, lay quiet and let it have its way.

I thought it probable that I was dying, and upon my word I did not care very much. I was so glad that I did not have a dog: I had wanted a puppy, had nearly bought him, but in the end I did not because long ago when my old Tory died I had sworn never to have another.

In these long silent days my mind revolved with a curious motion, slow and dispassionate, following no logical pattern. I said that there was hardly any doubt that I had deceived myself; that my passion was no more than the last burning-up of the desires of a man who, though long celibate, was still, after all, a male creature; that I had idealized a perfectly ordinary young woman by way of making my love reasonable—for a love like that, if it is not an illusion, needs a wonderful object—that I had taken Bronwen at her face-value and I was a poor judge of faces.

It was sad: yes; it was sad, but I was down below sadness now and the rain drove on the window and the evening went into night.

I was still all that night, quite still, and as far as I was doing anything—feeling anything—I was waiting. When you are waiting like that your face sets, and you do not like to change your face.

Emyr came in the morning. I heard him on the path with his dogs: there was Meg there and Taff as well as the terriers. I did not want to see Emyr. I do not know why; I had no distaste for him, no embarrassment or anything like that any more; but I did not want to see him or change the way my face was. He called once or twice: more, perhaps, but there was a good deal of wind—I would not have known when he went but for his voice far away up the road calling for Meg.

Peace came back at once; the wind outside isolated the house and I was there alone. The progressive detachment was almost complete now and I was waiting, but with no impatience, no emotion of any kind. Before this I had made some preparation for giving an account of myself. There were many, many things I had done for which I was heartily sorry, and many that I should have been ashamed to re-count; and I had led a selfish life. On the other side, I could claim to have been a fairly harmless creature: if I had not done much good, at least I had never had the opportunity for doing much harm. I hoped for a kind judge: I relied too much upon an unjust indulgence, for I hoped to shuffle by.

I was not afraid (physically, I mean): and as far as such a negative state can have a name I was content. Yet when I heard her voice calling, at once I rushed up through those peaceful depths, up to the surface of living and I called back, half raised in my bed. My voice was strange in my throat, another man's voice. And there was the pain again.

It was so quick. Days I had taken to sink down there, days and a resignation of spirit, and she had not reached the top of the stairs before I was there, on the old plane and my heart beating hard.

I would have slipped on my dressing-gown, but I was too weak to get up. It was mortifying to be seen like this, but I could do nothing about it. She brought me some milk, and I was sick. I was talking very much at random: the words and the phrases formed themselves and came out. I knew they were inept, but I was not able to control them.

Lord, how kind she was. She was alarmed by my state and flustered by my silly talk, but she had the situation in hand: no fuss; great kindness and good sense.

They brought the doctor. By a good chance Davies was away and this was a young locum tenens: he was an intelligent man. I liked him. The pain, by this time, was bad again and it was terribly exhausting to fight against it. I grew confused and could no longer follow the sequence of events. In the end I was down at the farm, in a bed in the front parlor.

It was delightful to lie there, after the first days, when young Morgan had coped with the pain and I had grown resigned to the idea of being a burden and an imposition. I lay there day after day in a kind of vegetable happiness: she was always there, or just at hand and there was no thinking or reasoning or restraint and I loved her. How can I express it? I loved her from deep down, with my whole being; but calmly, no striving, no pain. It was as if it welled up in me and overflowed. It made me so happy, so deeply happy—no, content, assuaged. I was as weak as a cat, and happy. God, I was happy.

I do not know why I should have been: I did not know then, and I did not inquire.

The room I lay in was a little, formal, triangular piece of the house, wedged between the staircase and the outside kitchen, the one in which they did the washing and messy jobs like plucking fowls and geese. The big kitchen, the place where the life of the farm was, lay the other side of the front door: there was a narrow bit of lobby just inside the front door and then the stairs; so I was separated from the big kitchen by a space wide enough to deaden all noise but sufficiently narrow to allow a diffused sound of living to come through, a murmur of activity that attached me pleasantly to life. I wondered sometimes why I did not hear the child; usually he cried or screamed or banged whenever I was there, unless they had already put him to bed. They had sent him away to an uncle's farm: that was typical of the kindness I found at Gelli. There was not one of them who did not seem pleased to have me there, planked down in their best room, eating their victuals, imposing in a hundred ways and turning their accustomed way of life topsy-turvy.

If I could single out one as especially good to me I should say it was Taid. He came and sat with me in the evenings and during the day on Sunday: we could not say much to one another, because my fragmentary Welsh did not reach him, and his English was limited to thirty or forty words, but we communed in our fashion. He would come in and say, "Is bettar?" and I would reply, *"Da iawn, diolch."* Short observations like that, which I could say correctly, pleased him very much.

Then he would sit stiffly in the upright chair and nod, or shake his head, while he worked to form the next sentence. There was such a goodness in him that it was a pleasure to have him by. I do not know how this strong, good impression was conveyed: his smile, perhaps, as much as anything; he had a saintly old face, and he was generally smiling, unless he was very tired. I loved to see him on Sundays when he was dressed in his black clothes for chapel: he held himself as straight as a grenadier and in his black broadcloth of antique cut he looked the image of a Liberal statesman of the great days. It was charming to see him when Emyr was in the room. He hardly ever spoke, but looked from my face to Emyr's, and when Emyr was speaking there was such pleasure in his face that no one could see it unmoved.

He and Bronwen were very good friends. There was no mistaking the affection between them, a quiet, undemonstrative pleasure in one another's company. I could not know him well, of course: we signaled good-will over a gulf, and even if we had had a common language we should have had little to say to one another. But I do not know that I ever met a man more worthy of respect and esteem.

I had always understood that the beliefs of his chapel were particularly harsh, adapted for a gloomy and unloving people, very far removed from our conceptions of justice and mercy. However that may be, Taid had drawn serenity from them, and he was a man at peace.

I saw much less of Nain. She was more timid; she would never come in and sit down, but twice every day she would come as far as my bed's foot and ask me how I did.

I never saw her without the idea of gentleness coming into my mind. The way she held herself, her quiet, hesitant voice and her lined, tired face—they were all very gentle. I think she had seen much more trouble than Taid, or had suffered more from what they had both experienced. She was small and slight—a curved feather, no more.

With all her timidity, she had a kind of fragile dignity that I had always admired: if one met her by chance, with a bucket of pig-swill in her hand, a man's cap pinned awry on her head and a torn sacking apron, she would always put her bucket down and talk for a few minutes with the same polite gravity that one found on Sunday, with her in her black silk dress in the parlor. She was always a little diffident because of her English, but there was always that air of breeding and a perfect disregard for non-essentials—old clothes in this instance; but I could think of many more. That natural, unconscious fine breeding struck me again and again; both Nain and Bronwen had it, and I had seen it (less marked) in other farms about our valley. When I was young, I was brought up in an ordinary English middle-class home in London; most of the people we knew either "went to the office" or belonged to some profession. We had no grand connections at all. But my aunt Theresa, who lived with us— she was plain and unmarried, but a dear—had a great regard for the aristocracy. She knew Debrett and Burke through and through, and she went so far as to study heraldry; she knew more about it, I believe, than many an armiger of seize quarters. How she relished its terms and the herald's names: she once met either Blue Mantle or Rouge Dragon, I forget which now, at a party in Hampstead, and it gave her more pleasure than if she had been presented at court, with feathers and curtsy and all. She had a very small income, but that little which she could regard as spending money went to form a library (after Debrett, Burke and Gwilym) of novels of a strongly aristocratic flavor. I loved her very much and when I was a little boy I took to her pursuits with enthusiasm; her values were mine at that time, and unquestioned.

She was not a snob. What she admired was worthy of admiration: for her a man of ancient lineage had the virtues of Bayard, as well as his glamour and panache. It was the virtue that she insisted upon, primarily, and she believed that if one were, by happy providence, born a de Vere one certainly should (and almost certainly would) behave nobly. I do not think that she ever met anyone whom she would have called an aristocrat (she was very severe on recent creations) so she died with her ideas unshaken.

Being a man, I went out into the world: not very far or deep, perhaps, but immeasurably farther than Aunt Theresa. I went with many illusions and I soon found them to be illusory. I did not hobnob much with the peerage, but at school, and very much more so at Oxford, a young man is brought into contact with others, some of them of very good family. With the best will in the world I looked for those qualities which I had been taught to expect, and I did not find them. I do not mean that these men were bad in any way; only that they were not better than the run of humanity, or at least not so much better that I could detect any difference. It is possible that I met an unrepresentative sample, but it was not until I came into Wales that I discovered the beautiful natural breeding that Aunt Theresa assured me was the mark of nobility. It was not common, but it was there; Nain had the manners of a duchess—a duchess according to Aunt Theresa.

I believe that my coming down to the farm did them all a great deal of good. That has an obnoxious sound, but I mean that the exercise of the purest charity brought out, or strengthened virtues in each of the four, and that they were the better for doing good. Certainly during the early days, when I was slowly getting better, it seemed to me that there was a complete harmony among them, just like that which I had thought to exist when I first came among them. Emyr showed at his best at this time: he shed those ways that I disliked—faults that I had had to search for, mostly. Though now that I come to think about it dispassionately, I am not so sure that I had been obliged to search for them: there were some that obtruded themselves, particularly his ruling in his father's house and a low cunning that peered out at the mention of money. But now he behaved so well: he listened until one had finished speaking, a real piece of self-discipline for him, and he seemed to be much more gentle with his parents. He took great pains to entertain me; he sat and talked by the hour, although he would have to work late for it, he brought me magazines and papers from Dinas, and all the time he seemed to be casting round for some new way to make my convalescence agreeable. I think he was gentler to Bronwen, too; or perhaps she was to him: but their relationship, although it was almost certainly faulty in some way, was a thing that I had never attempted to understand; I shied away from it.

It may appear strange that I gathered so much from sick-room visits. I had more to go on than that: I eavesdropped. Whenever the door of the big kitchen was open, as it was all day once I began to improve, I could hear all that was said there. I could not help it, and I told them that I understood more Welsh than I could speak. They did not exactly disbelieve me, but it was obvious that they thought I was mistaken. It was like Borrow's Spaniards, who spoke Spanish with him quite contentedly for days until they learned that he was a foreigner, and then refused to believe that he had more than four words of their language.

As far as my Welsh went, it was very far from being what Borrow's Spanish must have been, but I had been among them for some time now, and all the time I had heard Welsh spoken round me: one absorbs a language unconsciously; its accent, the fall of the stress and the timbre of the speech grow imperceptibly more familiar, and if one starts with a basis of grammar and a fair vocabulary a time comes when one realizes that a sentence has formed its meaning in one's head without any conscious effort, no catching and translating of the words, no re-arranging of the syntax to suit the English form. This came to me quite suddenly while I was lying there, my mind apparently vacant: it surprised me very much to find that I had seized the gist of a long and complicated conversation about the impending visit of one Pritchard Ellis, a minister. Some words escaped me, but the whole had conveyed its meaning as clearly as if it had been English.

The suddenness of my comprehension surprised me: it is true that long before I had been able to pick up the meaning of a good deal of what was said, particularly of short sentences called from one to another, but this was another thing altogether. It must have had a great deal to do with my physical state, because there were some days when I paid especial attention (days, generally, when I was feeling brisk and lively) and then the effort worked against itself: on those days I listened and the pattern of the sound seemed perfectly familiar, but somehow the meaning escaped me. It was as frustrating as a forgotten tune or a piece of machinery that has gone incomprehensibly and unreasonably out of order; you know that all the parts are correctly adjusted, the contacts clean, and yet the wheels will not go round.

The best time was when I was quite relaxed, lying comfortably and thinking of nothing, bathed in that mild euphoria that was such a delightful part of my life in that prim, incongruous little parlor, with its terrible best furniture and browning photographs: then the meaning came through, clear and effortless. Bronwen's voice always conveyed more to me than the others. I used to turn her words over, reforming expressions and phrases to use myself, holding imaginary conversations. They never were much use afterwards, but that was because of my faulty enunciation and a foolish timidity that prevented me from talking well even in English whenever I was not sure of being understood.

Bronwen spoke more clearly than the others, and she spoke a much purer Welsh—purer, that is, by literary standards. Her home was well placed for that: Welsh, as I understand it, differs very much in accent and dialect from one region to another; our valley was just the wrong side of one of these linguistic borders, whereas hers was inside one of the best for purity.

I told them, as I have said, and I assuaged my conscience; but I was glad they did not believe me. I should not really have expected them to credit me with any useful knowledge, for they had a low opinion of my understanding and of my common sense. It was not that they thought me uninstructed, far from that. All ornamental knowledge, the arts entire they allowed me; any dead or foreign tongue was mine, and a perfect acquaintance with all things past. But they would not trust me to tell the difference between a horse and a mare, and when I was pottering about the farm, they would send the boy to usher and guide me in any operation more complex than closing a gate.

Gerallt was at Bronwen's old home. Her brother (a pleasant, kindly little man, as far as I could tell from his intense shyness, but with nothing of Bronwen about him whatever) was much attached to the boy; he brought him over once or twice at the week-end, but for a long, peaceful time the farm was spared the howling, screeching and banging.

It appeared to me that Nain and Taid missed the little boy more than Bronwen; they spoke about him more often, and when he did reappear on these visits they were delighted, whereas her pleasure was more contained. These visits made me realize the value of peace. It was wonderfully peaceful at Gelli. Outside there were the farmyard noises, hens, ducks, the queer dry noise of turkeys, the horses in the paved yard, a pail being put on the flags and the clash of its handle falling after: generally there was the soft noise of the rain and the gutters running and sometimes when it had been raining hard all night the river in spate would be there, a great deep noise behind all the others, a noise that you did not hear unless the wind cut it off for a moment; as the wind blew, hard and soft, so the noise came, a breathing, then loud to a tone of menace. There were sheep always, mostly quite far, and sometimes cows, like organs when they were in the yard.

Bronwen used to bring her sewing in the afternoons: she had always used the deep sill of the parlor window—it had the best afternoon light—and once I was on the mend she took to it again.

Long, rambling, disjointed conversations we used to have. I do not recall what we talked about: it was very small talk, probably, but it was easy, unembarrassed and free. There was no sort of effort in talking to her. If we fell silent it was not that either was searching for something to say, it was just calm silence as companionable as talk. She had a fine gift for silence. How rare it is. I read somewhere that music is made up of the notes and the silence in between; the one as important as the other. It certainly holds good for talk.

She had no affectation; what she said was honest and ingenuous, and she talked good sense. When she thought before replying she had a way of looking straight into my face, gravely, as children do sometimes. It was disconcerting: at first I found it difficult not to smile back—hard to compose my face if we were talking about something for which a smile was inappropriate.

I came to know her then. All that I had supposed her to be she was, and more. There was character there, and strength, but a grace of mind beyond what I could have expected and—I do not know how to describe it—a purity, a quality of soul: but I lack the words for it.

We slipped at once into an open, friendly way of talking; closely, but well this side of familiarity. That was not the effect of reserve, still less that of awareness: on her side it came from a nature that kept itself a little remote from contact with other people. She had a world to herself where she was alone. For my part it was more conscious: I loved it so, and I would have feared any change.

I have looked over this last piece, and I am very sorry that it is so bald and inadequate: I have made her sound a prig. Nothing on the whole created earth could have been more essentially unlike Bronwen than a prig, yet I have described her as one. Try as I will I cannot convey what I felt with such clarity and strength. I am no poet.

Those days (I should have counted each one) were by far the happiest of my life. There were all the obvious causes for happiness, her presence, the sight of her beauty, her continual unfailing kindness—it was Bronwen who looked after me: if I begin to speak of her kindness, her perception and her delicacy while I was helpless I should never stop—and my great, confirmed, knowledge of her. There was the fact that I had been ill and in pain and that now I was getting better, and (here is bathos again) that Bronwen was a cook in a thousand, so that every day I ate more, with increasing enjoyment. But as well as that I had imposed a discipline on myself that allowed the happiness: before, I had made one of my own particular hells out of the thought of Emyr as Bronwen's husband; now, in the house itself, I saw that unless I could do something about it I should either go mad—I mean mad, insane; a mind gnawed hollow with jealousy—or harry myself into a physical wreck again, eat my heart out, as they say. So I closed my mind to that. It was not so hard as I thought it would be: if you turn yourself to it with the devil behind you you can build a wall in your mind that is very nearly impenetrable.

Pugh

=

It ended. Yes; but not before I had seized my happiness and known it. The man in Dante was wrong who spoke about the memory of former happiness. Afterwards I was able to escape from wretchedness to those tranquil days: those days when I filled myself with something that I had lacked all my life, something that gave me forever after a reserve of comfort, solace; a deep security. Events could shatter me still, and hope, despair and longing still would drive me to and fro, but now there was something down there, certain and unchanging.

The quiet pattern of life at the farm changed almost overnight; Gerallt came home, the farm-boy gave place to a new servant, and the minister came for his appointed visit.

The little boy's coming back (he was not a bad child at heart: I exaggerate) meant that Bronwen's time was taken up, that the noise in the house multiplied many times, and discord came in with him.

They did their best about the noise, all of them; but quite a small unreasonable noise is more irritating than the thundering of carts in a cobbled yard or the rolling of milk-churns. Some relative had given Gerallt a musical box. It was a metal object, about the size and shape of a tobacco tin, with a cranked handle. When this handle was turned a plectrum moved over a series of pins, which gave out different notes. The last two pins in the series were broken and the tune was forever incomplete. It was a tune something like Barbara Allen; one was left poised in the air, waiting for the notes that would resolve it all, and they never came. The beastly thing started again, and unless I paid attention my mind would follow unconsciously and there I would be, hung up, waiting and frustrated.

Nothing could have been much more trivial: the only excuse I can bring forward for my irritation is the crossness and the painfully acute hearing that so often go with convalescence.

The discord in the house was another matter. The grandparents were injudicious, very injudicious: they adored the little boy and indulged him excessively. His father did much the same. In all the farms or cottages I visited in Wales, in the shops and the village streets, I found nothing to contradict my impression that the children were spoilt, ill-mannered and noisy. Perhaps I am wrong in supposing this to be peculiarly Welsh; I had not lived in the country before or come into contact with children except in nurseries or presented, washed and brushed, to pay their duty to a visitor: in other farms and other villages I dare say the children bawl and scream, but I do not know it from first-hand experience. Still, Welsh, English, Irish or Hottentot, it is not pleasant to see a whole room full of grown-ups, old people among them, forced to shout their words over the din of one self-willed child, or to suspend their conversation until the brat chooses to stop its noise. It is kind of them to sacrifice their comfort rather than stop the child's enjoyment, but I am very sure that it is mistaken kindness.

Then I do not like being pawed with jammy hands; I hate to see animals mauled about like stuffed toys; I do like a child of a reasonable age to reply when I bid it good day; and I do not like to hear a parent flatly contradicted in a scream as loud as the child's lungs can make it.

All these things I saw continually up and down our valley, and I wondered at the patience of the fathers. I might go into a farm where I was known; I (or any other visitor) would be an honored guest at once—the best chair would be set, a cup of tea would appear, they would listen attentively and reply in the politest manner. Then some child would enter with a crash, glare stupidly, make no answer to my greeting, and start to shout for a biscuit. Everything would stop for the child: it would be gently reasoned with, coaxed and caressed. Eventually it would get its biscuit and with luck it might go out to torture a hen; otherwise it would stay, fingering one, staring brutishly into one's face.

They would do anything to make a visitor comfortable— fire blown, prodded, raked, cushions plumped, dogs and even cats driven out into the rain, the Derby cup dusted, everything except guard him from the assaults of the children. Where that was concerned they did not even feel that any apology was necessary: more than once I have been forced to smirk at a mother who was ineffectually holding a kicking little brute of five or six, smiling at me over his head as who should say, "Don't you admire his wonderful spirit?"

The children have no chance brought up like that. Even in the village schools the discipline is most imperfect: I asked once whether the master often beat the boys, and they told me that not only was beating forbidden, but that if any teacher were so hardy as to lift his hand to a child he would run a very fair chance of being paid in his own coin by the father, uncles, elder brothers, cousins—the whole tribe.

It is an ugly thing to watch, this spoiling and distortion of a child's character, but here it was, going on at Gelli. Poor Bronwen, she did her best, but against such odds she had no chance. Still, she tried every day, and I could never blame her when sometimes she was betrayed into vexation and spoke as she should not—as an ideal being should not, for I defy any mortal woman to see the teaching of her child systematically undermined without some angry reaction.

How many times did I hear her tell Gerallt to do something or call him from upstairs, and immediately afterwards hear one of the grandparents either call back to her or tell the little boy directly that he could do as he wished. Time and again the old man would give him something to eat from the corner-cupboard where the delicacies lived, or Nain would encourage some pretty insubordination. With the feeding out of time (they all did that) the child grew pasty and bilious, would not eat his meals and started a scene the moment they appeared on the table; the fractiousness of ill health was added to the natural childish bickering.

I think Taid behaved as he did from a sort of childlike glee; he identified himself with Gerallt. There was no trace of malice in him, but if he had deliberately set himself to wreck the gentle discipline that is necessary for a peaceful home with a child in it, he could not have done worse. He was sparing and austere for himself: in the whole year his only treats were a visit to Caernarvon fair after the hay and perhaps one visit to a big eisteddfod. He may have indulged Gerallt, as formerly he had indulged Emyr, as a form of liberation; but perhaps that is fanciful.

With Nain I could not tell: I thought, once or twice, that there was a conscious desire to go against Bronwen's wishes. And with Emyr it seemed to be just a general wish for immediate gratification, an unthinking siding with his parents and the child: it was very evident in the nightly scene about eating supper and going to bed. The protests one side and another would be punctuated with fondlings and those loud smacking kisses that I found so unpleasant—it is not a pretty sight, an unshaven man bussing a child's supper-smeared face. In the end the child would go off, far too late and usually screaming.

All that was ground enough for disagreements in a house, and although I did not think that I had come quite to the root of it, my mind was at rest as to the conflict between Nain and Bronwen. I had troubled my heart cruelly about it before, but a little while after I came down to Gelli I left off weighing, reasoning and deliberating about it. I abandoned reason: whatever Bronwen did was right; that was axiomatic. It sounds besotted, but it was not so blind. I *knew* that she could not be the coarse, hard woman I had suspected in my most extreme reaction. It was knowledge that did not require demonstration, though now my daily ears supplied me with it. A hundred times I heard her tell Nain that she would feed the pig, scrub the floor, fetch the water: the old lady would gently argue (it was mostly when Bronwen was already doing something else) and if Nain agreed in the end Bronwen would go on with her cooking, bed-making or whatever it was, and in a few minutes I would hear the clang of the bucket and Nain's slow, hesitating footsteps. Once, I am afraid, I heard the old lady, after one of these arguments, actually say to Emyr as he came in and met her, "Bronwen wants me to feed the little sow."

Then (this was more frequent later) I would hear her speak of Bronwen's things: but Bronwen never spoke of them so. It was countless trivialities that supplied my demonstration, the confirmation of my unreasoned stand: I cannot list them one after another, but the sum was that I heard Nain react (or appear to react) from illusage, but never once did I hear the unkindness which could have caused it. Never, that is, apart from Bronwen's rare, justified vexation over Gerallt.

Another thing that I was sorry for was the departure of John, the gwas. He had reached the age at which, by law, he had to be paid a man's wages, and Gelli did not yield enough for that. It had taken me a long time to get to know him; he was a stupid fellow, but not nearly such a dolt as he made out to strangers. He had a kindly, simple nature, and when he was not showing off he could say intelligent things about his work. There was that strange flash of poetry in him too, something that is not paralleled (I think) in any other country: he had been sent up once with the farm's big cross-cut to help me saw some wood, and while we worked (the movement and the noise covering his shyness) he told me the tale of the great sow of Môn and about an Irish princess in the

Lleyn, stories that must have come to him straight from the Mabinogion, or from the verbal tradition before that. He told them blunderingly in English, without any sort of affectation: I wish I could have seized them as they came from his mouth. Another time he told me stories that were familiar from my own childhood, though it took me some little time to sort the names from the Welsh to the English versions that I had known: Myrddin was Merlin and Cai was Sir Kay, but some I could not get. These were interspersed with garbled accounts of the films he had seen; they were equally contemporary for him.

That poetic insight, continuity, feeling, is as real as the mist in the hills. I could digress for a long time with great pleasure. A farmer from another land would not have said, as Emyr did, standing by the ripening corn, "It makes you want to take it in your arms, to smell to it: and to be with your scythe, so that it goes down with the noise. It bows as the scythe swings, isn't it, and it falls curved."

John went; he was to go to a farm in the plains where he would earn much more money and where there was a tractor, but he left sadly and cried like a child on his last night at Gelli: Bronwen heard him in his bed on the landing and comforted him for a long while, until he went to sleep. I could always tell when John was asleep, because he snored for ten.

He promised Taid never to drink or to smoke, and he was replaced by Llew, a younger boy from the village. Llew was not an attractive lad: he had a pimply vulgar face and something mean and furtive in his expression. He was a forward youth, always ready with his word, and he called me Mr. Pugh with every sentence. Still, he had an excellent character from the schoolmaster and he had been one of Mr. Lloyd's brightest pupils.

I do not know why I have not spoken of Mr. Lloyd before this. He was the most important man in the village after the chapel deacons, and as far as I could learn he was a most estimable person. His scholars were wild and rude, but they were said to be much better than those of the neighboring schools. He certainly had some very good ideas, and he did a great deal of voluntary work—evening classes, excursions, concerts, poetic contests. But I do not know how it was, we never seemed to find anything much to say to one another. We had met quite often and we had exchanged visits, but they were not successful. I consciously tried to be genial— fatal, of course, but the effort was necessary. He was always on the defensive with me, and would never speak freely. For many years he had been the only man of any reading, out- side theology, in the valley, and he had grown unaccus- tomed to the mildest form of contradiction. Once, in order to keep the conversation alive, in an attempt to inject some vitality into it, I had questioned his remarks about the purely Welsh origin of the harp, and he had thought that I accused him of lying.

It seemed a pity at the time that we did not get on, because he was a good man and he could have told me a great deal about the country and the people: but there it was, and I did not persist.

I retained a high opinion of him, though, and I remember with pleasure how often the boys and young men who had been his pupils spoke of him with affection, even the oafs and young ruffians like Rhys Llwyn, who stole my macintosh when I left the door of Hafod open one day.

Lloyd came to see me when I was getting better: practically everybody in the valley did at one time or another. It was very kind. It was ungrateful to wish they would not, and foolish, because if one wishes to understand a country there is no better way than talking freely to as large a number of the country-people as possible. It was the medical side of their conversation that distressed me: every single one had relatives who had undergone surgical operations or who had experienced troubles similar to mine. "The Gastric" in one form or another was a flail in the land and, I gathered, had decimated Wales. They described everything, especially women's innards, however disgusting (they are not disgusting to a farmer, I dare say), and they were damnably repetitious and long-winded. Lloyd did spare me that, and I was grateful; but he remained formal and reserved, and I had not the energy to make a special effort, so we remained on the far side of cordiality.

When the minister came for his visit he was brought to see me. I was sitting up by this time and he was almost the first visitor whose face I could see: all the others had sat in the stuffed chair with their backs to the window, and I from my bed, propped up and facing the light, had never been able to make out their features at all. This added very much to the strain of receiving visits: it is a strain to talk for any length of time in a foreign language; it is more of a strain to listen to people whose knowledge of your language is imperfect, and where any misunderstanding is offensive. In this case, if I misunderstood them it was particularly wounding, because of the link between fluent, correct English and social position. My difficulties, already grave enough, were much increased by my inability to follow the expressions on my visitors' faces.

I sound as if I were making fun of them: a page or so before I spoke in an off-hand way about their longdrawn talk of illness. I should have put it better, because I have absolutely no intention of slighting these kind people: they were really kind and good hearted. They were doing the Christian duty of visiting the sick, often at great inconvenience to themselves—and even expense, for they invariably brought "a little something," a dozen eggs, a great bowl of farm butter, cream, or some other delicacy. They would have liked the visits and the conversation themselves, and what other criterion is there?

Indeed, this whole piece, and what I am going to write about Ellis, the preacher, makes me feel uneasy and even dirty. The outpouring of dislike is ugly enough when it is spoken, but unpleasant things written about a man who cannot reply are graver and far more ugly. In any other circumstances I would keep these judgments to myself, but here the special considerations must be my excuse.

Ellis, then, came to sit with me, and I took an instant dislike to him. It was a dislike that started before the first words and increased with my knowledge of the man, and with all the charity at my command I still think it was well founded.

He was a little pigeon-breasted strutting man, black, with a lard-colored face. But what is the good of trying to describe what he looked like? Apart from giving his height and color—the passport details—what impression can I convey? I could labor at a description of his snouty nose and mouth, that air of self-satisfaction that survived every change of expression, his confidence, but even if my description were followed through its dry length, I am certain that the picture received would have very little resemblance to the original: there is no hope in my mind of giving the man as I saw him. One sees a man in a flash and one has judged him in a moment, the set of features, the body's stance, the taste of his personality, all at once; no prolonged list, however accurate, can give that instant effect.

In some bird books at the end of each article there is a feather-by-feather description of the bird: it is only with a great effort that one can connect the list with a living bird, and as for recognizing a particular species from it, that is quite impossible. The whole is so much greater than the parts, or rather the most important parts are intangible, not to be found in any list. Probably no two men worship the same God: I am sure no two sects do. We are given a certain set of qualities, a few specific but many more ambiguous, metaphysical, capable of a hundred interpretations. ("God is just": so is a hanging judge at the Old Bailey; so is a critic who is silent because he cannot speak truthfully without giving pain.) It is not to be wondered at if the deity invoked at a pontifical high mass is unlike that worshiped at a Salvation Army meeting—as different as the sound of Palestrina and the tambourine and cornet—no more remarkable than that a friend's friend, described by letter, should turn out an unrecognizable stranger.

I can only repeat that he was about five feet four, very upright and strutting, with a great deal of black hair and a glabrous, cheesy face (the skin was matt, no penetration of the light at all) with the snout and smirk that I have mentioned before. Obviously I disliked him at once and wrote him down a bad man, though at that time I had no reasonable grounds for doing so. For all I knew then he had never done a downright bad thing in his life (though from the first moment I would have sworn that he would stop at no meanness) and in all probability he would have done much good; but for me he was a *bad* character. It is very unfair, this dividing of humanity into good and bad. I think everybody does it: certainly for me the world has always been divided so. Perhaps it is a severe reflection upon myself that for me the bad division has always contained more than the good.

I have often wondered what it would feel like to be one of the other side. Perhaps it never happens; the whole world is on the right side, self-justification is so strong. There is Rousseau's saying, that every man is inwardly sure he is the most virtuous being alive. But how far down can that go? All the way to an atheistic parricide who lives by robbing the blind? Or is there a point where it must be abandoned, and if there is, what does it feel like after?

Of course, as we used to say so often in chapel, we are miserable sinners, and I know that in my life I did only too many things that I ought not to have done, and I suppose that when I did them I joined the other side—a joining that would have been obvious if I had been found out: but I never was and even at the time I imagine that I regarded these acts as exceptional, probably not wrong for me because of special circumstances, however condemnable they might be as a general rule. But even if they were wrong, and I admitted it in the doing, then I would have argued that they were but aberrations from a virtuous norm, and that once over (and undetected) I rejoined the unsinning sheep.

But the man whose daily life is evil, a hypocrite, can his justification keep pace? Or is he content to belong to the other side, and to compensate himself by a cynical appreciation of his own cleverness and success. I am speaking of a fairly intelligent man: for a stupid thief it must be quite easy—a brutish resentment against the world would suffice. I am speaking of Ellis.

Hypocrite unqualified is a big word, and I hesitate to apply it whole to Ellis. I think there were times when he was genuinely exalted by his extempore prayers and his hymn-singing and he may have taken that for religious experience; although I do not think he believed in God, a future life or the practice of a single one of the Christian tenets. But those moments of exaltation aside, he was Tartuffe to the life, and it astonished me that no one appeared to suspect this, in spite of his care. For he was very careful, very guarded. But he was not careful enough to keep his little pig eyes from running up and down Bronwen while they all sat, heads bowed, in the kitchen listening to him praying about the womb of the earth and the rains piercing its sterility, the seed and the ecstasy, and I sat watching him from the parlor, for they had left the door open in order that I might benefit from his unction.

In every human encounter there is a mutual probing, a weighing of the potentialities of the other. I was soon aware that this Ellis was very penetrating, very fine. He was an ignorant fellow as far as book-learning went, but there was a lively intelligence there, of a certain kind. I did not wish to be penetrated, divined by him: I kept at a distance, talking vaguely and sometimes foolishly: but when we came to our evening discussions, I found that he had exactly calculated my strength and my weakness as an adversary.

It was depressing to see the strength of his influence on the better people in the valley. Taid loved and respected him. The other deacon, old Lewis, Cletwr (very rich), came often to visit although the rivalry between him and Taid made Gelli an uneasy house for him, and it made me gasp to see this successful, hard old farmer hanging on the words of the Reverend Mr. Ellis. He was *revered:* there is no other word for it. The schoolmaster, too; he would get up when Ellis came in, though he must have been twice his age, and I know that he had a high sense of what was due to him.

I think that the base of Ellis' power must have been his pulpit oratory, but I cannot speak of it as I never heard him preach. I did not understand him well when he delivered those long monologues that were half sermons, because of the particular accent and special delivery that Welsh preachers use, and the unaccustomed turn of phrase, but they seemed to have a great effect on Nain, Taid, Emyr and any of the visitors who came in to hear him. From the style of these and from what I knew of the man I supposed that his full-blown preaching would be of the most enthusiastic hell-and-damnation kind, and I was not surprised when Nain assured me, with tears in her eyes, that at one open-air function he had converted eighteen quarrymen, who had been wicked before.

Bronwen did not like him. I was sure of that before I ever saw them together. I could not pretend to "understand" her thoroughly, as people say; there was much too profound a character there for any glib, facile comprehension, and in spite of the sympathy that stretched like a bridge between us, there were many of her reactions that were dark to me, and much that I could not seize. But as far as that went I was completely certain: there was no question in my mind at all. And I was right. She was very polite to him and I think she respected him for his calling; a mind as pure as hers could hardly in so many words grasp the existence of a spirit wholly depraved: she suspected it then, I believe, but deep down; and she certainly turned from him with an instinctive aversion. Why was this aversion not more general? These people were not fools; they were not to be imposed upon in other ways. All that I could bring forward, different religious traditions, love of oratory, success (he was very successful), the power of example; these did not seem to me to be enough. But obviously they were: I did not understand it.

It was necessary to keep on civil terms; one must not start quarreling with the friends of the house, and in this case more than any other I would have done anything rather than disturb the peace of mind of my hosts: it was Taid in particular that I thought of; that good old man's tranquillity—it would hardly have been an exaggeration to call it holy. He never suspected my loathing for Ellis: he was charmed that I should now have someone to talk to. "We are ignorant men," he said, "like sheeps."

It was fortunate that I should have had a good deal of practice in living sociably with people I disliked, because Ellis regarded my reserve as a challenge, and he would not let me alone. An invalid is very helpless, and although by this time I was walking about quite easily, up to Hafod and back for books with no great effort, I could rarely escape him; the wintry spring kept me indoors nearly all the time.

He soon found that I was not to be charmed, and then he tried to dominate me: at least I think it was that. He was always driven, he had to be proving his defenses by attack: I know that he felt that his reputation was at stake.

Whenever there was an audience, and there often was—Taid, Emyr and myself sitting round the big kitchen fire, with a visitor or two, and the boy Llew on the settle in the background—he would start some discussion or other, a point of doctrine, the superiority of the Welsh over the English (he was a prudent Nationalist, the depth of his dye depending on his company) or some political measure. He was a clever fellow: he knew exactly how to trim along with the opinion of his people—implied flattery of the audience and all the rest of it—and he always chose to talk on subjects with which he was well acquainted, like theology, or, if he strayed out of his narrow limits, to confuse it with irrelevances and cloak his ignorance with a cloud of words. He knew by this time that I knew what he was at, but he spoke for victory in the minds of his audience.

It is possible that he had a commonplace material motive as well: as I understand it appointments among the nonconformists depend on the favorable opinion of the elders; and Ellis was ambitious.

In these discussions there was no place for the liberal exchange of ideas; they were contests, nothing more or less. I was an unwilling participant most of the time: in the first place I did not care for being in the same room as Ellis, and I did not wish to be a party to his designs. There was no escape, however, without giving offense where I could not bear to give it. They loved these evenings, the others: Taid would sit beaming from one speaker to another, jerking his head in a very knowing fashion, and occasionally he would say Very good. Emyr would whisper a translation to him from time to time, otherwise even the general drift would have escaped him. Between translations Emyr sat with his mouth open and his face shining, enraptured: had we been two Solomons we could not have given him more pleasure.

In talk of this kind, with such an adversary, a man is shackled who has some regard for truth and civility. When we talked about Wales, for example, I could not bring forward instances of the nation's bad side, not sitting there before a Welsh fire, a guest in a Welsh house. But Ellis was at liberty to vilify England as much as he liked, and free to make what accommodations he chose with fact; so he usually had the best of it. Although I knew that victory on these terms did not wholly satisfy him (he was too intelligent for that) and although I knew that often I was possessed of arms that could have crushed him if I had chosen to use them, yet still my vanity was sufficiently engaged for this to be irksome. It was petty of me, I know, to have been irritated by such a fellow, but I was: there were little things that stuck in my gullet, the snigger of Llew when Ellis scored a point (he was all ears, that boy, and he listened so intently that he dribbled), the unashamed partiality of the audience, and Ellis' insufferable habit of touching me to emphasize his argument. Beyond that I must admit that he was a much more facile talker than I was; he had a glib flow of words and images that I could not but admire, however little I respected it.

What really vexed me was the presence of Bronwen. The women took no part in the talk; they hovered from time to time at the edge of the lamp-lit circle, but they never sat down with us. Before I understood this barbarous convention I had embarrassed them both by offering my chair. Still, they were there, and I was sure that Bronwen followed the turn and run of the argument. A man must be of a bigger nature than I was not to wish to shine a little, or at least not to be overcome, when his—what, sweetheart, beloved? mistress?—is there.

I did have my little triumphs, though. Once or twice Ellis' caution slipped and he talked of things he did not understand. Greek poets, once. He knew some New Testament Greek, but nothing of Attic, and I indulged in the pleasure of making him look a fool; he disguised it very ably, but I knew he was writhing, and I kept it up for some time. And once I was able to knock his degree of Bachelor of Divinity on the head with my doctorates, but that was ignoble and gave me no pleasure on reflection. He was eternally jealous of my different education and standing, and he could not refrain from taking notice of it. His usual way was to try to make me appear to take a stand on privilege—a mock humility: "Of course, Mr. Pugh, I have not had your advantages," or "But I dare say they know better than us at Oxford, isn't it?" It is a difficult attack to parry, but the spite was a little too evident; he overplayed his hand, and sometimes he made the others uneasy.

Only once did I really beat him down. It was one of those tedious, interminable harangues about the wrong-doings of England. I was quite identified with England, despite my Welsh ancestry and name; and seeing the poor old country so abused I accepted the nearly untenable post of defender: I say untenable because I defy any man to defend the actions of Henry VIII against his grandfather's people, or that series of repressive enactments that ended in the decay (now happily arrested) of the Welsh language and culture. The conversation followed its well-beaten lines (the past is close at hand in Wales, nearly as close as it is in Ireland) and diverged to treat of the English kings.

I have no strong political opinions: if most of the Liberals I knew had not been vegetarians or holier-than-thou water-drinkers, milksops, I dare say I should have been a mild Whig. But as we came down through the generations from the Georges through the old Queen to our day, and as the manner of speech showed a kind of disrespect that I could not tolerate, I felt myself growing more and more Tory every minute. I was becoming seriously displeased. Ellis did not see it until he had gone too far and he was shocked and surprised when I cut right across one of his treasonable periods and put him to silence.

My words may not have been very impressive; I stuttered before bringing them out and said, "Mr. Ellis, this conversation is in the poorest of taste. It is most unpleasant to me and I must ask you to stop it at once. We will speak of something else, if you please." No, I could have improved on the words if I had not been so angry; but the manner was effective enough.

He stopped dead and looked frightened for a moment. There was an uneasy silence in the room, broken only by Llew's snigger. Ellis darted a look of hatred at him, and I began to talk about the charms of life in the country after many years of life in the town.

Bronwen

Q. Mr. Pugh came into Cwm Bugail after Gerallt was born, I think?

A. Yes, long after. He came to Hafod the year we lost all the hay.

Q. What did you think of him at first?

A. I did not think anything much about him at first. He seemed a good, quiet sort of gentleman, but I thought he was just one of the English visitors who would go away very soon. He came the autumn before, for a holiday, and then he took Hafod for good the next year. Emyr saw more of him, and liked him very much.

Q. Did Emyr like strangers usually?

A. No. Particularly not English visitors. There were Welsh people from the university who used to stay in the village— Nationalists. He liked them. He liked talking to them.

Q. Did it surprise you that he liked Mr. Pugh?

A. I do not remember now. I don't think so: anyone would have liked Mr. Pugh.

Q. Mr. Lloyd did not.

A. No. He was jealous because Mr. Pugh was a professor at Oxford or something: but Mr. Pugh always spoke well of *him.*

Q. Emyr did not mind Mr. Lloyd's opinion?

A. Oh, Mr. Lloyd never said anything; he was much too good for that, and I do not think Emyr ever knew—he did not understand people very well. If they would have used hard words to one another he would have understood, but not otherwise.

Q. So Emyr liked him?

A. Yes. He was always asking him things and Emyr would tell him. Emyr liked that. He used to tell Taid what Mr. Pugh said, and they laughed, because Mr. Pugh did not know the difference between a hespin and a wether. It was not that they made game of him, but they could not understand how a man could be so ignorant. It pleased Emyr to explain things to a college professor, but besides that Emyr was a kind, friendly man if he was spoken to properly, and he liked to be a good neighbor.

Q. At first you did not see much of Mr. Pugh?

A. No, only when he came for the milk, and a few times when he came in for tea or supper when he had been out with Emyr on the mountain, to see the sheep or for the gathering or something like that.

Q. You had no very clear impression of him?

A. He was always very nice. He treated Nain and me like ladies and took his hat off when he came in and said Thank you for a very good tea, or Thank you for a good supper when he left, and he brought a present for Gerallt, a teddy-bear, from London. But although he came down more as Emyr and he grew more friendly, he was just the English gentleman at Hafod, and I put half a pint of milk aside for him every morning. I did like him, though I did not think of him much beyond the milk. When he looked poorly I put cream in the milk. It was not until he fell ill and came down to stay with us that I came to know him at all well.

Q. How did that happen?

A. He had been looking ill for some time, Nain said—she saw him more often than I did when he came down in the morning. Then for some time he did not come down at all and we began to get frightened for him. Emyr went up, but he did not seem to be in, and he came down again. Then I went up, carrying the milk, and I thought I heard him answer when I knocked, but it was blowing hard and I was not sure. The door was on the latch and I listened inside, and there he was, calling from upstairs. I went in. It was such a mess you would not believe. He was in bed, with a muffler on. He was so pale I thought he was dying. He had not shaved for a long time and that made him look even worse. I thought he was dying, and I was so sorry and put about. But he answered sensibly and said it was very kind of me to come up, but I should not have bothered; he said he was quite well, only a little cold. I asked him if he could take a little something, like some warm milk, and he said he was sure it would do him good, but I was not to trouble. I went down to the cegin-fach behind: the mess was terrible. Dishes everywhere, piled in heaps, and on the floor. All the saucepans were dirty. There was no kindling. It went to my heart to see

it. He had a patent stove, but I was afraid of it and lit a little
fire of paper, just enough to heat the milk. When I brought
it to him he started to drink, but he was sick before he could
finish it. He was so ashamed of the mess, and all the time I
was clearing it up he was apologizing and his voice got
weaker and weaker. At the end he was hardly right—he was
talking so that I could not understand him. I tucked him fast
into his bed, because he was moving his arms about, and ran
down. Emyr went for the doctor and Nain and I went up
again. He seemed to be asleep, so we left him and began to
set the place to rights.

It was dreadful. He had no more idea of looking after
himself than a baby. He had more plates and dishes than we
had at the farm, for all of us and for the shearing, and he
had used them all. There was mold on some of them; and
mice everywhere. He had never swept once, I believe, since
Megan Bowen had stopped going to Hafod. There was nothing in the larder except dozens of ends of bread and some
cold fried eggs. The doctor said it was the gastric, very bad,
and it turned out that he had eaten nothing but eggs for
months and months and they were very bad for him: he did
not know how to cook anything else.

The doctor wanted him to go where nurses could look
after him, but the cottage hospital was full, and he did not
like to send him the long journey to Llanfihangel. In the end
we looked after him for two days and then he was brought
down to the farm and we put him in the little parlor.

It was then that I got to know him well: Nain and Taid
could not understand him much when he spoke English, nor
when he tried to speak Welsh—the words were right some-

times, but it never sounded like Welsh—they could not understand it, and Emyr was out most of the day, so I had to talk to him most.

Q. When did you know he loved you?

A. I don't know. Not for a long time.

Q. Had there ever been any talk at Gelli about Mr. Pugh admiring you? Even in joke?

A. No indeed.

Q. On your side, when did you come to think lovingly of him?

A. That was a long time too.

Q. It did not happen suddenly?

A. Oh no. It was slow, slow; I do not even know when I first thought of it. I liked him so much as I came to know him: more and more every day I liked him.

Q. What made you like him so?

A. Oh, everything.

Q. But what special things?

A. Well, it is hard to pick on things by themselves. His kindness. He was so good to Taid. There was that time when Rhys, Llwyn, stole from him and he would not have him locked up although the sergeant was very angry about it. He said he would deal with it himself: Rhys said he gave him a pound. Then when Pritchard Ellis came and they used to talk in the evening: they were all against him, and he answered so well. Pritchard Ellis tried to bait him but he never said anything, never flew out, only answered gently, and made Pritchard Ellis look like the mean cunning low thing he was.

Q. Can you think back to the time when you first began to wish that he might distinguish you?

A. I must have answered stupidly. I never did want him to trouble his head about me for a moment. I liked him very much—everything he did or said, practically, and the *way* he did or said it—and I was sorry for him, because he was sad and alone, with nobody. But as for wanting him to look twice at me in that way, no it never could have come into my head. I never put myself to have any man pay court to me in my life: and in those days, a woman as I was, I would not begin to think in that way.

Q. I did not mean to offend you: believe me, I did not intend any offense. Let me put it better. You did love him in the end, did you not.

A. Yes. I loved him dearly, and before the end.

Q. What I should like to know, then, is when you began to know the strength of your feeling for him. Was it in response to his affection, or did it arise before you knew his state of mind?

A. It came so gently, little by little, I cannot tell.

Q. When it did come, and you knew it, did you not think it very wrong to love another man besides your husband?

A. No. It seemed to me quite right.

Q. Was that because of your unhappiness with Emyr and his mother?

A. If it had all been quite different, if I had been happy, I do not know. I would have been a different person without those years. But whatever I might have been I am sure I should have loved him if I had known him in the same way.

Q. I think we are using the word for different things?

A. Yes; perhaps.

Q. It would be best if you were to tell me how things happened after he came down from Hafod.

A. He came very ill, as I told you. We sent Gerallt away to my brother: it was Taid and I who thought of it, to save the noise. Emyr and Nain did not like it at first, but they said it was right afterwards.

Q. A moment, please. What were your relations with Emyr and Nain at that time?

A. They were better. Then when Gerallt was away and we were all anxious about Mr. Pugh we all drew together much more. Emyr was very good: he was really upset, and he would have done anything, only there was nothing he could do.

Q. There was none of that trouble with Emyr?

A. No. There had not been for a long time.

Q. So things were all well at Gelli then?

A. Yes. While he was ill, the time when he was getting better, but before Pritchard Ellis came, were the best days I ever had there, except for a little while after Gerallt was born. We were all friendly together: there was a good feeling in the house. I missed Gerallt though; he had never been from me before.

Nain was kind to me: she knew I missed Gerallt and she was kind on purpose. When there was not Emyr or Gerallt between us she might have been my mother, she had such a good heart for me. At that time she did not mind my things in the house any more, nor my cooking.

There was another thing. It had been a bad year, rain for the hay and the corn, and the foxes had had a great many of the lambs: then the prices at the Grading had been very bad. The cows were the only thing that did well that year, and they cost such a lot in the winter. We were all troubled for the winter. But when he was beginning to sit up and read books he asked to see Emyr. They were together a long time, and I heard Emyr say, No, oh no, you are very welcome, Mr. Pugh. He came out looking very happy and said to Taid that they could write off to Lincolnshire for the hay now. We were very sorry we had to take it, but it was the only thing (he could not have borne to be a burden) and it was such a help. Emyr gave Nain and me a new winter coat each. You would never have known he had done it: he always behaved just the same, like a friend we had asked to stay, not a visitor—not a summer person, I mean.

Those days seemed so good and natural, not like something that was good but could not last. I used to sit with him in the afternoons, and we talked. If I had been clever I would have known how he felt, but I don't think I did at all, at that time. We talked like friends. There was none of that air with him—do you know what I mean, jokes and a way of speaking? It was not him a man and me a woman.

Q. What did you talk about?

A. All sorts of things. Anything that came into our heads. I had never had anyone to talk with like that since I was a child. He knew a great deal, but he never talked as if I did not understand. Mostly we talked about quite ordinary things. I told him about when I was a little girl at home and about the old things my father had told us. But even when we talked about nothing much it seemed to be very interesting.

He spoke sometimes about his life before. He had not been very happy. There were some funny ways he had: he spoke like a grandfather now and then, as if he was very old. He was not very old, anyone could see that, but he was afraid of being old and he talked as if he *was* very old. I would tell him that he was quite young—not flat out like that, of course, but so that it did not show. It did please him so.

Q. What sort of an impression would Mr. Pugh have given to women in general?

A. Nothing much at first, I don't think. He was tall and much too thin: he did not stand up straight. He was not handsome. You would not notice him at first. He had a sad face, except when he was talking. He was very quiet, and he had beautiful manners, but until you knew him quite well you did not notice that—they were not party manners; they stayed all the time. Afterwards I used to be surprised that I had not noticed it before, how nice it was to see him smile.

Q. Then Mr. Ellis came. What difference did that make?

A. It was not only Pritchard Ellis. Poor little Gerallt came back too, and he was more spoilt than he had ever been. It was a queer thing that Meurig's wife should have been so good to him; she had meant to give him a good holiday, not to spoil him, but it came to the same thing. It was strange, because she had never liked me, and Meurig had said over and over again, when she was there, that in time Gerallt should have the farm—you would have thought that would have put her against him, but it did not.

He was becoming a very disobedient, self-willed little boy. He was still as good as gold at heart, but there were times when I wondered if it could last, and what sort of man he would be if he went on growing that way. My heart went cold when I thought of what it might be, Emyr being his father.

At first I could hardly do anything with him, and he made as much noise as ten. I was very unhappy that Mr. Pugh should see him like that, because I should so have liked to show him at his best, and to be proud of him.

It started the old trouble again. Nain and Taid were delighted to have him back, and if I checked him even a little they thought I was cruel. Soon with Nain it was "Bronwen says this," "Bronwen says that," "Don't move the settle, because Bronwen will not like it."

Then Pritchard Ellis came. There was much more work to be done, and whatever I could do Nain would be scrubbing the floors or carrying the water. I wondered what *he* made of it, and what he thought of me.

I think Nain began to stop liking him then. If I wanted Gerallt to behave well and be quiet it was partly so that he would be spared the noise—I did not see nearly so much of him then, but I did see that he suffered from it; he looked very pale sometimes, and I am sure his head hurt him—and so she began to wish him away.

Q. Tell me about Mr. Ellis.

A. Where shall I begin?

Q. Start with how you came to know him, what you thought of him then, and how he came to be visiting you.

A. He was a famous preacher, a relative of Mr. Lloyd yr Ysgol, and he had always come to stay with him in his holidays when he was a young man, before I married Emyr. Every year at the chapel they had him to preach, and then he would stay with one of the deacons. This time he was spending a long time with us, because he had left his old place in the south and he had to wait before his new one was ready. I do not know why he did not stay with Mr. Lloyd, but it was arranged long before that he should be with us. Taid was very pleased: he honored Pritchard Ellis, and loved to hear him. He was a famous preacher.

I had heard of him before coming to Cwm Bugail, but being Church at home we had never seen him. The first time he came to stay for his preaching after I came I did not know what to make of him; it seemed that I could not be right, with the others and everybody in the village and in the papers saying what a fine man he was. He was very polite to me.

The next time he came I still could not be sure, but when he came this time I knew I did not like him.

Q. Why not?

A. I just did not like him. He was like a slug.

Q. Did you have no other reason than that?

A. Well, his airs. He was always very neatly dressed in his black. He took great care of his clothes and he shaved every day. He never dirtied himself with work; his hands were white and rather fat, like a lady's.

He would come and watch the men at work, but he never took off his coat, though he had been born on a farm. He was so sure that he was right that nobody minded or took notice, even when every hand was wanted, like at the threshing. It was very different with Mr. Pugh: *his* coat was off in a moment and as far as he knew he would help in anything, however dirty. He took no notice at all of his clothes. (When I went through his washing after he came down from Hafod I found he had not one whole pair of socks—he bought new when the holes were too big—and he had safety-pins where buttons had come off.) He never could help much, although he had such a good heart, because he did not know how to handle anything. He did his best. I have seen him as pale as death carrying a little ewe that the gwas could have swung with one hand. He did not know how to use his strength or how to handle any tools. You have to be born to it. Pritchard Ellis was born to it, and he could have done it easily, if he had had a man's heart like Mr. Pugh.

Q. So those were your reasons?

A. Yes: I know it was wrong to think like that of a minister, but until I had good reason to stop I respected him. You can dislike a righteous person, but still respect and listen to him.

Q. No, I did not say it was wrong; I only wanted to know the order of events. Please go on. You had come to your reasons for ceasing to respect Mr. Ellis.

A. I saw him with Mr. Pugh. He hated Mr. Pugh for being what he could never be—oh, he was mean and envious. They used to talk in the kitchen after the day's work. I knew Mr. Pugh wanted to talk peaceably and friendly with everybody, but Pritchard Ellis always turned it into a thing like those debating societies they have. He did it to show off and to work his spite on Mr. Pugh. You could almost see the spite oozing out of him.

Often Mr. Pugh did not want to talk at all; anyhow not like that; sometimes he was feeling ill, and they kept him up in that stuffy room in front of the fire until I thought he would faint. He did not like to stay in his room: he was very careful about giving offense, and he knew what pleasure it gave Taid and Emyr to hear a discussion. He was so much above Pritchard Ellis. One thing showed it very well. There was the best chair: Taid sat in it on Sundays if there were no visitors. Mr. Pugh had always sat in it every time he had been in our kitchen. Pritchard Ellis was never quiet unless *he* was sitting in it: when the chairs were being put for the evening he would hang about near it so as to be ready to dart into it. Mr. Pugh never took any notice at all: you would never have known there was a best chair. Pritchard Ellis would look so triumphant and mean.

Then when they were talking I knew very well that Mr.

Pugh could have put him down many and many times, if he had chosen, but he did not, from politeness or just not troubling with him. If it had not been our house he would never have had two words with a fellow like Pritchard Ellis. Sometimes they talked about things we had talked about when I was sewing, and I knew what he could have said if he chose. I have seen Pritchard Ellis seem to make a fool of him, because he did not choose to answer what he could have answered. He let him do it, rather than offend the others who were listening—they were talking about the Welsh and English.

Once or twice he let Pritchard Ellis know what he could do if he cared, and once he stopped him just like that, like slamming a door, because he was saying bad things about the King. He would not allow it to be said, and Pritchard Ellis never said another word—looked like a hang-dog thief. Oh I was so pleased to hear him at last. I could have hugged him.

He properly frightened Pritchard Ellis: he was afraid it might go further and spoil his respectability. He made the others promise not to say anything, afterwards: he said he was just testing Mr. Pugh, for a joke. He liked to dandle with the Nationalists, but he wanted none of their risks. He had never gone so far. It was his spite that had pushed him, although he took such care.

Q. You must have loved Mr. Pugh by that time, I think?

A. Perhaps I had begun then.

Q. Go on about Mr. Ellis.

A. There was another sort of much bigger reason. Pritchard Ellis was bad. I had begun to suspect it because of something I found in his room. Then I knew it because he made a

rat-hole bigger so that he could look into our room at night:
I think I found it the same day and I moved a trunk against
it; but it made me feel dirty all over.

He touched me on the stairs—we were alone. I hit him so
hard that he gasped: even then he was careful not to make a
noise. I wish I had marked him. I would have killed him if I
could. I hit him with all my strength. It made me cry, I felt so
dirty. It was like having been smeared with a mess all over;
even inside with filth.

Q. Did you tell Emyr?

A. No. I thought about it. But the fuss—then he would
have denied it. And he was going away soon. No, I did not
tell anybody. I would not have told Emyr in any case. There
was no telling with him. He might have killed him, or it
might have started him again. I could never trust poor Emyr.

Q. How did Ellis behave afterwards?

A. I was never alone with him again, I took care of that. He
was not afraid; he knew I would not tell. It did not stop him.
I saw his face when he looked at me. I know he left the dirty
things in his bedroom on purpose so that I should see them.

He went to spend the last week at Mr. Lloyd's. It was a long
week before he left. I hated to see him touch Gerallt, playing
with him. I hated to hear him praying. It was false and
wicked when you knew what was inside, and sometimes I
understood him—the sense beneath, I mean—and it was
disgusting to be there. When he was in the room I did not
like to breathe the air that he had breathed. He was a bad
man: the worst I have ever known.

Q. I want to go off onto another point. You changed servants at that time, did you not?

A. Yes, I forgot to say that. John went to Mr. Davies, Ysgubor. I was sorry to see him go. We had had better boys, but he was a good one. He had reached a silly age, and he went to the cinema too often, but he was a good, loving boy really. I often thought of him when Llew came. There was not anything you could like in Llew. He was clever and he did his work well, but you could not like him like the others. Pritchard Ellis might have been something like him when he was young.

Q. To go back to Mr. Pugh for a moment. He did not like Ellis, of course; but did he dislike him very much?

A. I believe he disliked him as much as he could. But Mr. Pugh was so far much better than Pritchard Ellis I do not think he could hate him properly. He would never have understood how bad and rotten he was.

Pugh

===

When Ellis left it seemed to me that the house had more air in it, it was a healthier place; one could breathe freely.

It was too much to hope that the peace that he had spoiled would return at once, but we did have some beautiful days that I love to pass through my memory.

Bronwen and I were very close at that time. There was an understanding between us that arose from no words, gestures, or looks. There was a curious side-shoot from this; time and again after a silence she would say the words that had already formed in my mind, or she would hum a tune, coming in at the bar that I had reached in my interior song. Sometimes I would know exactly what she was going to say and (what was stranger) what I was going to reply, so that I heard my own voice running over the words already familiar. This was a queer, disturbing feeling, something dreamlike.

It had never happened to me before; but then I had never loved before, with my whole heart and soul.

We were alone one day, one of the first windless, sunny days of the growing year, and I had brought my chair out to the lovely green under the ash trees. A stream ran deep along the edge against the plough, and there was the continual music of it in the still air. She joined me with a basket of darning, and all the long afternoon we talked. I love to dwell on this time, because I re-create my happiness and because while I am in it I need not go on. Perhaps it is out of place to record a conversation like this: it has no direct bearing on anything. But irrelevant or not, I am going to put it down.

We were talking about the world at large. I said that I thought it was in a bad state, steadily getting worse: she thought that it was a good place for people to live in, and that it was getting better and better. She said she did not know anything much outside her own life (it was not false modesty; it was a statement of fact, and said like that) but even in her life there were so many things that were better already. There were anaesthetics (the blacksmith had pulled her first grown-up tooth), operations where it had been death before, physic for the sheep, the injections for the cows, health insurance.

"When I was a little girl," she said, "my brother had appendicitis, and my father sent for the best doctor he could. He was a surgeon from Liverpool, staying with Dr. Rhys. My brother was very bad (it was sudden) and the surgeon came that evening in the trap from Bettws and Dr. Rhys with him. They did it in the kitchen, because the light was best there. When it was all over and they had had a cup of tea my father asked what he owed the surgeon from Liverpool, and he said sixty guineas. My father thought that he had not heard right, but he had. Dr. Rhys said it in Welsh. He paid down the money in sovereigns, and never said anything. Afterwards he said what did it matter compared with Meurig's life or his health: he said nothing matters so long as you have got your health. But for weeks and weeks after he looked desperate and pale. It was within five pound all that he had been able to save, and all his safety. It was not the money that was costing, it was the sheep on the mountain and the life of the farm. It was not right like that.

"A hundred years ago my brother would have died, and even twenty years ago it could have ruined a family; now it is the ambulance comes, and a few days in hospital and it is over."

"Yes, there are many improvements like that, and they are very good things, excellent; but I meant it in a more general way. You can cure some of the worst injustices, but you cannot get at the base of the misery. Indeed, you might say that everything that keeps people living longer or helps to increase the population really makes the misery worse, although it seems to be good in each particular case.

"It is in towns that you see it most clearly, but it is really the same everywhere. Always, all the time, men are forcing themselves to do what they do not want to do, and keeping themselves from what they do want to do."

(I write this as though it had been a monologue: it was not, entirely, but it is a convenient form.)

"Have you noticed that man is the only unhappy animal? and that the more complex the society the unhappier the man? Imagine living in an American industrial city. But even in good conditions, where do you find a happy man? A man happy in the ordinary course of his life, without some exceptional, temporary cause. In our days you find him in a madhouse.

"I think it can be explained like this: we are an evolutionary mistake. We evolved too quickly, and now with the instinctive equipment of apes we are faced with a social life as complicated as a beehive. Men cannot live that kind of life; it cannot be done, and I am sure the attempt will kill us as a species.

"The root of the unhappiness is that man's instinctive sense of right clashes with that of society: and it is not surprising that it does, when you consider the speed of our evolution. Only a little time ago, a very little time as these things are reckoned, man was a comparatively simple creature living in small bands. He had reached this point by the ordinary very slow development and of course he was suited for it by the necessary set of instincts. His ideas of right and wrong would have been based on what was good for his band, a small group made up of his family. That right and wrong would have allowed for a great deal of what we now call selfishness, but it would also have called for courage and devotion for the sake of the group—for his own small group only, not any other group.

"Then at some time, the Fall, with the forbidden fruit, our queer lopsided intelligence came in, with all that followed—fire, tools, weapons, the conquest of other creatures, agriculture, the enormous increase in our numbers, and farewell to happiness. Men breed slower than almost any other creatures, four or five generations in a hundred years—there are not so many generations between us and that time. There has hardly been time enough to grow a single new instinct, or to discard an old one. So now we must face this ant-hill, beehive of a life with the old set of instincts hardly altered at all. Everything that we have that is new has had to come from outside, learned from experience and reason: it all has to be learned. No child starts life with language or the alphabet. Every man begins as a little ape; his hair grows so that it will shed the rain as he squats; his hands will swing his new-born body if you give him a twig. If he were left alone he would obey the laws suitable to his ancestors' condition, but he would be an impossible member of our present society: he must be made to conform (as if he had to be squeezed into the carapace of an ant), he must be taught the right and wrong of a social creature and made to obey it by all the force of example, education, public opinion, all the imaginable substitutes for genuine social instincts.

"All this, law, religion and all, is not enough to beat the old Adam. To obey the code that his education and his reason tell him is right for his present state, a man must perpetually cross and thwart the first, instinctive wish that rises in him. There was Confucius: he says that it was not until he was seventy that he could obey his impulses and yet do what was right. It was not until he was seventy that he could be entirely happy. If it takes seventy years for a very wise man, how long is it going to take for an ordinary man? He is never going to manage it. He is in continual conflict with himself, and he is unhappy. An unhappy man dislikes himself and his fellows. This unhappiness has been going on from the earliest historical times: our whole history is a tale of unhappiness, with war following war, each crueler and bloodier than the last, until in our day we wipe out a hundred thousand with one bomb.

"There is continual war within the nations: for every detected crime there are hundreds unknown. The very existence of laws proves the need for more and more control, and proves the little value of the control. The crime goes before the law, and how many laws are there now, in our country alone? No one can count them.

"No; I am sure that it is the natural way for a mistake to wipe itself out. The poor thing has grown mistakenly and he is unhappy, so he will come to an end. (Countless thousands of other kinds of creature have done so before him—extinct for other reasons, but evolutionary mistakes just the same.) He will multiply and multiply: he is bound to that now, but as his progress grows faster and faster so it becomes more and more impossible for him to be what he must force himself to become.

"I suppose the end will be a violent one—it looks very much like it. But if it is not, then I suppose he will taper away into the unknown, from despair. Already you see the birthrate falling in the advanced Western countries. Once they pass a certain point of misery, creatures stop breeding. It may seem strange to speak of the more advanced countries as more wretched than countries where famine and pestilence are there every day, but it is just because of the advance that the real misery is greater—the difference between what a man is and what he is made to be is greater. There, in the barbarous countries the enemies are obvious, they are external enemies that can sometimes be beaten. With us the enemy is inside each man: you can beat famine and disease in the end, but while you remain a man you cannot beat the ape."

Bronwen, after a silence, asked me how all that fitted with

a man having a soul, and I said I did not know. It was something new that I had been thinking about, and I had not yet sorted out all my notions. I thought that I was right then, in the main, and that there was nothing in this that was irreconcilable with another concept of man's nature.

A cold wind sprang up, blowing off the somber face of the Saeth, and drove us indoors. The gwas Llew was there—I had the impression that he had been hanging about for some time—and our talk was finished.

The others came home shortly after. The men had been to a sale of cattle and the old lady had taken Gerallt down to see a family of cousins: I turned in quite soon. I had some letters to write, and anyhow I did not feel equal to talk that evening.

When I was in bed I thought about our good, peaceful afternoon and I wondered why I had been talking as I did. She had taken it all in her stride, but it was not a suitable kind of talk at all. Was it just the pleasure of opening my mind without restraint? That was a real enough pleasure, and there were few people I had known to whom I could talk in that way, saying freely whatever arose, however foolish, without any contest or pretense or desire to shine. I wondered whether the search for hidden motives was really worth the trouble, and whether one did not perplex the issue by overmuch subtlety. Was it better to leave one's subconscious mind alone—take the motives at their face value—or was it better to pick at it with unskillful fingers?

Leave it alone, was my answer, and leave the *gnosce teipsum* to wiser men. But still I wondered. I had not meant to show off, I was sure of that. Was it true that the whole tendency of the discourse was to undermine her faith in religion, to debase man to the level of the brutes, and to shake her ideas of right and wrong. Was there any truth in that? I rejected it with indignation. With too much indignation? I knew very well what it meant in my case when I said that every day a man had to force himself to do what he did not want to do, and to keep himself from doing what he did want to do. And I knew what had made me so unhappy for so long, so desperately unhappy. In these quiet days I did not suffer as I had, not a thousandth part, but I wanted her, always. I wanted her, in spite of all the discipline and the barriers that I had put up in my mind, I wanted her with a longing that went right through me, as strong as a man can feel.

I wanted her physically, too; I had no doubt of that. When I was a young fellow and had my few little fluttering affairs, timid affections, I was ashamed of wanting any of the girls I admired; it seemed impure and wrongful then.

I drifted off my train of thought as I grew more sleepy and I let images form in my mind as I used to do when I was a child: there was the picture of her head, bowed over her work with the dark mountain behind, she was listening closely and there was that queer moving smile on her face. I smiled too at the memory of it—I felt the smile come on my face in the dark.

After he had left the farm Pritchard Ellis had gone to stay at the schoolmaster's house, and I heard that the day before he left he preached a sermon that was very much admired: from what I heard it had been about the sin against the Holy Ghost. I did not think much about it, except to regret that the simpler days of thunderbolts for blasphemy were past: I was heartily glad that the valley was free of his unclean presence.

But the slime that he left wherever he went did not disappear with his going; whatever I may have hoped. Even a fortnight after I had said good-by to him (with as hypocritical a smirk as I have ever summoned up) I felt that it was still there, poisoning the atmosphere.

Apart from that one day I hardly saw any more of Bronwen. There was something wrong in the atmosphere; there was something lacking that had made that good feeling of community in the house. It was hard to analyze, and I could not put my finger on it. The daily round, the meals, the casual talk, it seemed to be all the same, but there was something lacking, something essential; but I could not tell what.

What was more disturbing was that their attitude toward me seemed to have changed. Or was I imagining that again? They were as polite still as on the first day I had seen them, in spite of the familiarity of our life. No: I was sure that the old cordiality had gone. Nain was different, and probably the others too. I churned over a hundred far-fetched causes: was I giving too much trouble, eating too much, making extra work? Was I a bore, a restraint? Did they resent their lack of privacy? Had they seen that I disliked the child? Surely not: I often played with him; and really he had a sweet ingenuous side when it was not overlaid, when he was not being rowdy and unpleasant—and I would have borne fifty times the noise without complaint because he was his mother's son.

I even, for one chill moment, thought that my love had been discovered—talking in my sleep, some romantic nonsense of that kind. At the very beginning, the year before, I had been afraid of my shadow, terrified of betraying myself; I had felt that it must be written on my forehead for all to see. But after a few uneasy weeks common sense had returned and I knew that it was my secret. My guards had become instinctive; the manner of my love was rare. A love without words, looks, gestures, no outward life at all, who can tell of its existence? I had never thought of it again until that moment, and now the thought rested only long enough to be rejected.

" 'Whoever guesses, thinks or dreams he knows, Who is my mistress,' " I said, "must be a man who has dived into my heart, a man of supernatural powers." And I dismissed it forever. That, at least, I did not have to fear. There were plenty of other less fantastic things to weigh.

The house was changed; and I would have given my right hand to change it back again. There was the difference in Emyr. He was distrait, almost hag-ridden. He had always given me the impression of being a very nervous man, liable to excess of delight or despair; he had none of his father's serenity. Now every morning at breakfast I saw him silent and brooding, his eyes rimmed with red as if he had not slept; it was painful to see him come from the depth of some unhappy thought and put on a smile to say good morning or to answer a trivial remark. It had been a bad year, I knew, and I thought it might all be caused by worrying about money.

From what I had learned by observation and inquiry, I had gathered that all these mountain farms were worked with the minimum of capital, often with less than that, so that a couple of bad years in succession would bowl them over or plunge them so far into debt that it amounted to much the same thing. In addition to this chronic lack of capital, they relied on sheep alone for their money. The other things came more under the heading of subsistence farming. So if the sheep did badly, everything went; and there were so many ways for sheep to do badly. There was disease and bad weather to begin with, then the causes quite outside the farmer's control, the international price of wool (an abundant shearing in Australia could be the deciding factor in turning a struggling Welsh farmer off his land) and the market for lamb and mutton.

I talked to Emyr about these things in general; he confirmed what I had thought, and I told him that at that time I had a certain amount of free capital that was doing nothing (it was quite true: I had sold out a block of Rio Tintos for the purpose) and that if he chose to make use of it he was very welcome. I suggested that the money should pay interest if and when it made profit, and I flatter myself that I sounded reasonably businesslike and avaricious. I told him also that I was a man alone in the world, with no relative nearer than a second cousin—a man far richer than myself—and that I had thought of leaving Gerallt a life interest in my little fortune before it went to my old college.

I said that this was by way of a thank-offering for their kindness to me while I was ill; that it could not cause me the remotest inconvenience, as I should necessarily be dead before the act could have any effect; and that it made no difference to my college, which was already six hundred years old and which would (God willing) last another six hundred easily, whether it received my trifling addition sooner or later.

My conscience in this was perfectly clear. I wish that all the actions of my life had been as unmixed. The first idea was to make things easier and less worrying for the farm. The investment (and I knew I should not lose by it) was something from myself to Emyr as a man, a man for whom I had a real esteem: Emyr as Bronwen's husband did not enter into it for a moment. By that time I had succeeded in making a pretty rigid division between them. It would cause me no trouble of any sort, for I was living well below my income, and there was even money lying idle in my bank. As for the second idea, it was one that had been in my head for a long time. I would have done it anyhow, without speaking of it, but it followed naturally in the conversation. It was more selfish, perhaps, because the boy (disagreeable though he was) was Bronwen's son, after all. But what I had said was true, and a sufficient motive: in such a case it was not so very wonderful—certainly not disproportionate when one considers how very little it must mean to me after I was dead who had my money.

Emyr's reactions surprised me. He had not spoken much while I was talking, which was strange, because he had, to an advanced degree, that damnable habit of interrupting which you generally find in nervous people. He was very much embarrassed. He brought out his stumbling expression of gratitude with difficulty and an utter lack of grace (I had noticed before that he could not say thank you freely, and it was a trait that I regretted) and although I saw a real pleasure in him, a grasping at the idea, I was almost certain that basically he wanted to refuse the money, both the one and the other.

I had not expected that, not for a moment; particularly as he had owned that nothing would be more valuable to the farm than an extra thousand pounds of capital (I had mentioned twelve hundred): there were the current needs and a whole list of obsolete or worn-out equipment to replace, as well as new things, draining, reclamation and re-stocking.

We left the things in an unsatisfactory, undecided state, hanging in the air, and I went to bed very disappointed. Before our talk I had nourished the comfortable vision of myself as the Fairy Queen, my offers received with glad cries; and that was quite shattered. Perhaps it was fitting; but it was a disappointment.

This all happened after supper, in the parlor. I went to bed directly afterwards, and I heard them talking and talking in the big kitchen until well after midnight.

I had a strange dream. It was one of those dreams that you read—a printed page is the image—but at the same time you are not a detached reader; you are the person about whom you read. It was a very clear, complete dream, beginning, middle and end all sharply defined: it ran—

"He woke suddenly, completely; he was clear awake at once from a bottomless sleep. It was entirely dark and he could not tell which way round he was. With his two arms stiff behind him he sat up, propped up, listening. Why was he listening, and what room was this? He moved, felt with his hand for his pillow; it was not there: he tried—a separate effort—to remember the lie of the room (what room?) and where the light was. How extraordinary not to see any hint of light, no undarkness to betray the curtains. It was as if he was blind. Was he blind? He had heard of a man who had been blind in the morning, from a syphilitic gumma.

"He held his hand in front of his face and his staring eyes focused: the warmth of its nearness he felt, but he saw nothing.

"There appeared to be no wall behind the head of his bed.

His tentative fingers stretched out and out into the darkness. His body was waiting. Yes, but why? And why was his mind tense? Tense to breaking, I mean?

"He did not move again for a long time, waiting for the tension to die and for everything to clear, fall into the recognized pattern: but still there was the darkness pressing against his face, pressing in all round, crowding him.

" 'Well, I'm damned,' he said at last. Was he damned? Yes; he was damned for ever now.

yes he was damned for ever now for ever and ever now for
    ever and ever damned
yes he was damned for ever now for ever and ever now for
    ever and ever damned
yes he was damned for ever now for ever and ever now for
    ever and ever damned."

And so the pages ran, turning fast, the print diminishing to footnote size, smaller, faster the repetition forever faster and the speed was terrifying.

In the morning my propositions were accepted—gracelessly on Emyr's part, I must say—I gave him my check and we worked out a system of accounting. It was unnecessary for me to insist on its not being an obligation, but a profitable business deal, a speculation on my part; Emyr saw to that.

With Taid it was very different. The good old honest man was frankly delighted. He smiled and laughed like a man with a great impregnable wall between himself and the enemy who had been at his throat. He held the check with endearing admiration; he said he had once seen one for eight hundred and thirty pounds, but never one like that, with four figures. If it had not been for their ingrained love of secrecy I believe he would have shown it to his friends; but in that country matters touching money are kept silent, always, though there is an intense curiosity about them.

He shook my hand for a long while, lovingly I might say, and he said I was a *good* man. It is pleasant to be treated like that, and I almost forgot my disappointment.

The women were supposed to be out of this; it was not their province. They knew, of course, but it seemed to me that Nain was puzzled and undecided whether to be happy or not—now one, and now the other. Bronwen was charming, dear Bronwen; but there was something, some alloy, I could not tell.

In the end, when it had shaken down into perspective after some days, I asked myself whether I was glad or not and I decided that I was, certainly, if it was only for the pleasure of seeing Taid happy.

But I could not understand the others. I seemed to have distorted the old fabric still more, where I had wished to restore it. It is true there was a greater deference and a wish to please: but if I had purchased that, I had not bought back our former peace.

Lloyd

═══════

"Now, Mr. Lloyd, would you tell me about your cousin, Mr. Pritchard Ellis?"

"Yes indeed: there is no man I would rather speak about than Pritchard Ellis. I was very proud to be related to him and to have been able to help him at the beginning of his career.

"I have heard many preachers, but none to touch Pritchard Ellis. He was younger than me, but for years before that I had looked up to him. There was a sad time in my life when I was tempted with doubts, and he solved them for me: after that time he was always my spiritual adviser, and if ever I had any difficulty I went to him. He was very much in favor of confession as it was used in the primitive church, and he encouraged anybody to come to him for advice. He was a great comfort to Emyr Vaughan, I believe.

"He was as modest as could be for himself, although he

had a high respect for the character and dignity of a minister. His life was very pure, and he expected other people to be as pure as he was; if they were not, he did not spare his words. The most terrifying sermons I heard him preach were on the occasion of some impurity that was discovered in Llanfair, when there was mixed dancing there.

"Sometimes he told me privately of the terrible things that went on in the Rhondda when he was minister there—it might have been the cities of the plain, it was so bad—and he said how painful and disgusting it was for him to have to go into such things.

"As you can imagine, he was very much respected in our valley, being so famous outside it. He could have had his choice of a dozen pulpits at any time, and we considered ourselves lucky to have him to preach in our chapel once a year.

"He was a long-suffering man, slow to form a bad opinion of anyone. He often told me how much pain it gave him to believe evil of any other person. But once he had made up his mind he was firm, very firm. He had not made up his mind about Mr. Pugh until just before he left Gelli and came to stay at my house. He told me the first evening, with great sorrow (he was very much disturbed), that he was forced, against his will, to find that Mr. Pugh was a wicked man.

"I was shocked to hear this and I asked him why. He would not tell me for some time and then not until he had offered a prayer.

"When he got up he said, 'That man is carrying on with Bronwen Vaughan.'

"I did not know what to say; I could not find any words to answer. He went on, 'The woman is an adulteress and the man who calls himself Pugh is a fornicator. There is terrible wickedness at Gelli, and perhaps we do not know the worst.'

"I said I hoped he might be mistaken; but it was just something to say. I knew how sure he must have been to have said a thing like that. Then he told me how he knew. He had suspected it first from their way of talking and he had watched them. There were a great many little things he had seen: she was always the one to go into his room, and she always shut the door behind her; when she came out she would be smiling and happy, whereas she was rather sulky as a rule (I had noticed that, too). She was always correcting Gerallt in case he should annoy him with his harmless play. 'We should never trust a man who does not love little children,' Pritchard Ellis said. There was her rudeness to Mr. Ellis because Mr. Pugh did not like him: Pritchard Ellis was very fair; he said that he did not mind the rudeness—we cannot command our likes and dislikes, and she had never liked him—it was the *cause* of the rudeness. Then he said he knew that Emyr was not happy, not happy in his marriage, for certain reasons. But that was not enough; that was only the beginning. He had still hesitated, but then he saw them together. He told me exactly what they did; it was terrible. I do not know how it came about that he saw them; he did not like to speak of it any more, and it was very delicate, indeed.

"He said it must be stopped. I asked him how; whether Emyr should be told, whether he would speak to Mr. Pugh or Bronwen? He said he was not sure yet. He would think about it while he was away, but before he went he would preach a sermon in the chapel about the sin and the damnation that certainly followed it unless there was repentance in time, and he would pray that any man or woman guilty of that wickedness in Cwm Bugail might repent before it was too late. He said if that did not answer before he came back he might be able to find another method then—he was to return for his annual engagement in a few months.

"Later he said he would have a word with Armin Vaughan and Emyr, not to tell them what he had told me, but to see what was in their minds and perhaps to suggest to Emyr a way of teaching Bronwen her duty.

"He saw them the evening before the sermon, but I do not know what he said. Emyr looked very strange, I thought.

"The sermon. He had never preached with such fire: it was terrible to hear. He began by a long silence, and before he spoke he groaned: very quietly he began, but when he reached his denunciation his voice was so loud it filled the chapel. He always used a great deal of action in his preaching, and when he came to the torments of adulterers in hell it was like a drama: the people were groaning, and Mrs. Evans, who had been rebuked twenty or thirty years before, was crying nearly to hysterics. I looked at Bronwen's face. It was dreadful to see that she was not moved, not moved at all by such goodness for her; such a hardened sinner not to be moved by such unction and delivery. She looked to be thinking of something else. He was more than two hours preaching. At the end he was exhausted and went to bed at once after tea: he had to get up early in the morning for his train.

"One thing that had surprised me when at first I reflected on the terrible thing that Pritchard Ellis had told me, was that I had never until that moment heard any whisper of it. I never listen to gossip, of course, but these things fly about a village, and a man in my position hears everything, whether he wants to or not.

"It was because they were so secret, no doubt, and they had the perfect opportunity; if he had not been lodging there it would have been noticed long before. Or perhaps it was that I had not paid enough attention before: it was probably that, for a very little while after Pritchard left I did hear rumors. It was Mrs. Kate Williams, Yr Onnen, who told my housekeeper that they were doing it.

"There were many other things I heard too; she had left the farm in the middle of the night—that was when he was still at Hafod. She had been seen with him in the haybarn; he was giving her presents from London. There were many, many things that I heard.

"The feeling in the village was strong against her; that was to be expected, she having been so proud.

"Nobody knew whether they knew at Gelli. None of the men would have asked Taid or Emyr for their lives, but I believe some of the women went to see Nain. But they got nothing out of her: they had always kept themselves rather to themselves at Gelli, and they lay well out of the village, so there was not that coming and going that there would have been if it had been a house in the village, and of course not so much information.

"Some pretended to know more than they did: I heard it repeated that Emyr would not attack him for fear of scandal, and would not make him go away because he paid so well— it had been a bad year for all the farms. Some said that Nain knew but would not tell Emyr. Mrs. Evans said that Bronwen was expecting. Many of them thought that: she looked poorly.

"I wanted to know what was happening there. Armin Vaughan was my old friend, and Pritchard Ellis had solemnly asked me to write to him to tell him what happened, so that he could judge the effect of his sermon. Because of that I considered it my duty to listen to the gwas, Llew, and almost to encourage him to come and see me. He was a sharp boy, and not much escaped him. He said he had known it before Pritchard Ellis, and he had seen them many times; he thought they were still doing it.

"I wanted to know the truth, and I asked Megan Bowen, who had obliged for Mr. Pugh at Hafod before they parted on some disagreement. She was a stupid woman and she knew nothing about it. She said it was all nonsense, and if she caught anybody saying that about Bronwen she would give them a knife to eat: I believe she would have; she was a very rough old woman. Every Sunday Bronwen carried her a hot dinner, so I suppose that was why she knew nothing. It was strange, though, because she did not seem to care for Mr. Pugh: she said he was a poor, thin fellow. It was no good talking to her; she was a queer, independent woman, hardly respectable except she was a widow with a good pension.

"It went far and wide. I heard it in Llanfair and Dinas, and Dai Jones wrote to me from Liverpool to ask if it was true what he heard there. It is natural for people to be interested in one another's affairs in the country, and anything of that nature was sure to be talked about: but this time there was much more talk than usual. It was because Bronwen was such a strange beauty for our people—I do not say that for myself, for I never thought her more than very pretty when she was younger, but other people who were better judges said it was so and no doubt they were right in their opinions—and it was because the Gelli's had always held their heads high. Indeed, one of the saddest things about all this was the pleasure all the people in the village took in the misfortune of the Vaughans, and their hope that it would soon be worse. Even good men and women who had known them all their lives would clack their tongues and say it was very sad, but in every way they showed how excited and pleased they were. It was not that they wished them any harm. I am sure that if there had been a fire at Gelli every one of those that said bad things would have been there to help, or in illness, they would not have been wanting in charity. It was this particular thing.

"The women, most of them, had never liked Bronwen and for them (and for the men) it was worse because she was going with the English gentleman. There were a lot of bad things said about him: they said he came into our country with his airs and ways and he thought everybody else was dirt. They said he would not have left his own country if he had been good enough for them, where he came from. They said he had insulted the rector down at Pontyfelin: nobody had much to say for *him,* but at least he was a Welshman. They said that his name was not Pugh at all—he only put it on to sound Welsh: but I am sure that was not true. They said he had quarreled with Mr. Skinner, Tan yr Onnen, who was a man with a big house and servants. They said he ought to go back to his own country, before he did something else in the valley. They said there would not be a blessing on anything in Cwm Bugail while he was there in his sin."

"Was there no one who said anything the other way?"

"Yes. There were some, Megan Bowen for one—she said there was no truth in it at all, but she was a stupid woman who would contradict anything. She said to Henry Watson, the English lorry-driver, who had passed a remark at Williams' sale rooms, 'I am castratting those—s if they are talking.' She knew the word because of the lambs.

"There were some men who said that he was not so much to blame, even King David had done it, and of course the young men and bachelors were not judging him. A few women, too, who did not blame him so much because they said he was led on: but that was not the general feeling. It was strong against them both, but strongest against her.

"You had only to point out the dreadfulness of the crime to the others for them to admit at once that there was nothing to be said.

"I did not know what was happening at Gelli. I often met Emyr and Armin Vaughan, but I could not understand anything from them. It was queer, I could not talk to them the same as before; it was as if something had changed. It was almost as if I had done them some wrong and I could not properly face them. Other people were like that too. I did not think Armin Vaughan knew anything about it, or what people were saying, but I could not tell with Emyr. He was strange with me. I could not tell, or talk to him properly to find out. It might have been so many things, as well as the awkwardness between us.

"The others I never saw, Nain or Bronwen and Mr. Pugh. I did not go there. I felt I could not.

"It went on for week after week, and the excitement went on. It did not get less. The women were all on about Bronwen expecting: she hardly ever came into the village now—she never had much, but now they said she came much less, ashamed to be seen and afraid of what they might say or do—but when she did come they all ran to look, every one of them, to see if she showed.

"They all used to ask the grocer and the baker after they had been there delivering. It took them twice as long on their rounds with the questioning.

"I did not like it. I never did say that wrong was right, but there got to be a time when I hardly knew my own mind. It was the women outside my window: they went clack clack clack, never stopping. There was the servant Llew; I was afraid that it was all doing his character great harm and that I should never have listened to him. I had to check him; it came to me that I saw that he took a nasty pleasure in telling me what he saw, or what he said he saw, because I was beginning to doubt him.

"Then, when I was disgusted at the clack-clack-clack I asked myself whether I was not one with them. It was a bad thought, that. Pritchard Ellis reassured me in a letter and exhorted me to continue with my duty, but still I turned from it. I had never doubted him before, but I thought he might be mistaken now, at such a distance. There was something *nasty*.

"I thought I would go to see Mr. Pugh. I was not sure what I should say to him; I hoped it might come while I was talking. I wanted to do what was good in that family: but when I was halfway there I thought of his clever talking and his way of talking and I turned back home.

"I was sorry, and ashamed for my weakness, and when I was in bed I thought what I would say. The next day I took that road again, stronger in my mind but still doubtful and hoping that it would come with talking.

"The first person I met by the cattle-gate said, 'Bronwen Vaughan Gelli has poisoned herself.'

"The second person, hurrying on the road, said, 'Bronwen Vaughan is poisoned.'

"I did not speak to them. At the farm there was violence and disruption. One of the carthorses was clattering lost about the yard. The little boy Gerallt stood with a white face. Llew the servant was whispering close to Gwyn Davis and inside the house someone was going Oh oh oh. I spoke sharp to Llew, told him to put the mare away and set the farm to rights. He could hardly obey me; he could hardly think of work, like a dreadful holiday.

"The doctor came out of the house. She was dead. I went home and all the way there were people hurrying; but I could not speak to them."

Bronwen

Q. So it was better when Ellis left the house?

A. No. There was a short time when I thought we were rid of him: I turned the house out like another spring-cleaning, but it was no good. He was still there in the village and Emyr went to see him. Emyr was very queer after that. I thought I knew him through and through, but I could not understand him then. He was very good and gentle with me and he wanted us to be like lovers again. He was forcing himself to it in some way; he had never been like that before; and although he was so gentle I felt something behind it: he was keeping something back and it was against his nature.

Q. You refused?

A. Yes. It was no good. I could not think of it. I would have liked to be kind to him, but I could not trust him. I knew it would be the end, for him too, if he started again.

Q. Was there any thought of Mr. Pugh in your mind when you would not have him?

A. Oh no. I had reason enough without any more. But perhaps knowing him, having him in the house, made the thought of Emyr worse.

Q. No words had ever passed before this between you and Mr. Pugh?

A. No. We had never said anything; we never did.

Q. But by that time you knew how he felt, and how you felt for him?

A. Yes. But we had never spoken; there was no need. It had taken me longer to know his mind, but before that, long before that, I loved him.

Q. Why was it so long, do you think? He had been breaking his heart for you a great while.

A. I was stupid, to begin with. When you are all taken up with everyday work you do not notice things that you would not look for. I would never have looked for Mr. Pugh, whether he liked me except as the woman of the farm. If it had been, say, Dai Hendre Uchaf wanting to make court to me I dare say I would have seen it as soon as he did, or even before he knew his mind, and I would have sent him along at once. At the very first you can do it without hurting at all.

Q. Had you been obliged to do it before?

A. Oh yes. There was Trefor Williams—but it was not important. It was just his way with every woman who was not old. And a few others when I was a girl. It did not matter, once I understood how to send them away.

Q. Yet with Mr. Pugh it was so different? He was a man like the others, surely?

A. It *was* different, though. We were only common people, working people, and he was a gentleman coming from England. For us it makes a great difference. They can be very nice to us, friends even, if they are what my mother called the real gentry, but there is always that big difference. Unless you are like us you do not know what a difference it makes, shaving every day and putting on a collar—just that, without all the rest, being educated, knowing foreign countries and being rich.

Q. Did you count Mr. Pugh rich? He lived in a cottage by himself and he had no car.

A. Yes. He was what we call rich. He did not have to work.

Q. So did you think of him as a superior being?

A. Better than us? No. It was not better, exactly, though he knew so much more and he had such fine manners. Not better or worse. It was that he was different. Just *different.* I do not know how to explain it better than that.

Q. I should like to go on just a little longer with this point if I may. I understand that he had many different ways, another way of talking and behaving, but he was still a man like every other man, was he not?

A. No. He was not a man like any other man. He was the dearest man in the world for me. The difference in him was right inside, nothing to do with him belonging to other people. Without his gentry or his money or anything, if you put him by another man it was gold against brass. But to begin with it was just the ordinary difference that made me so slow and stupid. Unless he is wicked (which you can see at once) you do not expect a man like him to admire you.

Q. Would it not be flattering?

A. Yes, it would be flattering for a—for a bad woman.

Q. So there you were, with love for him. You cannot fix a time when it began?

A. No. I have tried. Perhaps it was some time before Pritchard Ellis came. It was somewhere about that time when I felt it in my heart, a great comfort, like something that gave me strength. When I knew it, and said it to myself, then it began to grow fast. The sound of him moving in his room was lovely. The smallest thing. And then I quickly knew that he was the same for me. It was good, so good that there is no way of telling how good it was. It was music in my heart. I cannot say what it was like, but I know that I would have gone through anything, *anything,* Emyr and all those years for it: it was worth that and a hundred times over.

Q. Did you intend to do anything about it?

A. Run away with him? Like that?

Q. Yes. Or anything else, as people do when they love one another.

A. No. If it had not been for Gerallt and Taid it might have been different. But dear Taid, he knew so little about anything, and he was so happy, and it would have broken his home. He loved Gerallt even more than he loved Emyr. It would have broken everything in his life, all the things he had longed for and worked for so hard: he had reached them at the end of his life.

There was Gerallt—he was *theirs* altogether; who could steal him from them? But to leave him to be spoiled, and worse than that, with no one to make him into a good man? With all their love they could not do what was right for him, and I had a dread that the bad part was creeping into his nature, although he was so good as well.

Then I had a duty still to Emyr and Nain. Without me the

house and the poultry and geese and accounts would have gone into a wreck. That was what I owed Emyr, to keep his house and to help working the farm together: and to Nain, some kindness.

There was no leaving, you see.

As for the other thing, yes, if he had wanted to. I would have done anything at all to give him pleasure, but I would not have been much for him, I had been hurt so, and turned.

Q. You would not have thought that wicked?

A. No. But that is all on one side really. He would never have wanted me in that way.

Q. But he did want you, very much.

A. I am sure he thought so; but he did not really. He had all sorts of ideas, but by his nature he did not do anything. I am not saying anything bad against him; no one could say anything bad against him without a lie in it somewhere. It is much better to think and talk beautifully than to do almost anything that is done. No: that was his nature, and it was the best nature ever made. But if it had really come to that, if I had said anything, he would not have wanted it truly, in his heart. He would not have been afraid; no, he had all a man's courage, I know he had, but he would not have done anything of himself.

So I was content to be as we were. We were happy. I wished for nothing more. Even if he had gone back to Hafod and I had only seen him on the mountain far off I would still have been happy.

Q. When you say that he would not have done anything, do you mean that he would not have loved you, as people say love, or do you mean that he would not have gone away with you?

A. No, I do not mean that. He would have done both, but it would have been against his nature. It would have been me urging him—even the very smallest bit, it would have been me, not him.

Q. I do not quite understand you. Why should he not have acted for himself?

A. He could have explained it so well. It was like this: he *thought* about everything. He turned it round and thought about it and saw all the things that were to be said on one side or another. Hardly anything was plain and simple for him as it would have been for me. And then in the end when he had thought a great deal he would put it down and do nothing because he would not take upon himself to decide what was best. It was his nature, like it is the nature for one tree to grow straight and another to keep low and spread into a tangle.

Q. Would you say he was ineffectual?

A. Not if it meant anything unkind, or would hurt him. I would not have anybody say anything against him; nobody, however grand. I have never told you enough how good and kind he was. He was so much better than I have been able to say.

Q. But if he would not decide about something very important, or would not act on his decision?

A. It was not that, exactly. I wish I could explain it better.

Q. Could you have relied upon him?

A. Yes; I would have relied on him to the end of the world for truth, and doing right. If he did not make his mind up to do things that was not his fault. It was not weakness in him. It was his nature, and if it had been different he would not have been the same person.

Q. Would you have preferred it if Mr. Pugh had had a more decided character?

A. No. I loved him exactly as he was. You can love a man and even his faults—it was not a fault in him, but even if it had been I would have loved it because it was part of him. But I know I have explained it badly.

Q. No, I assure you I understand what you mean very well, and I do not intend to say anything against Mr. Pugh. But just at this point I should like to ask you a question that may sound foolish. What did you call him?

A. I called him Mr. Pugh and he called me Mrs. Vaughan when he called me anything—usually he did not.

Q. Did you call him Mr. Pugh privately, to yourself?

A. I think I did. Yes, I suppose I did. But if I said "him" to myself it meant Mr. Pugh. We did not have any need for called-names, and I think it would have come awkward. Even when we talked Welsh (we did sometimes, a little) it was *chwi,* never *ti* as you say to people who are close to you.

Q. Now we come to the time after Ellis had gone right away.

A. He never went right away. The day before he left he preached in the chapel about adultery. I went because Taid wanted me to go. At first I thought perhaps he was reproaching himself for his wicked thoughts; I almost said that he was not as bad as I had thought—he had more temptations than a married man. Then I understood him, the coward. I was able to govern myself and shut my ears to him; it was easier after he began to speak about God, because I would not ever allow myself to listen to him talking about God ever since I had understood him at Gelli. He shouted and banged there in the chapel, with his pale face sweating; I thought he would never come to an end. The people said he had been wonderful; such *hwyl* had never been heard in our chapel, they said.

I did not know for some days how they had taken it, or whether they knew what he meant. I think Nain did from the beginning, but I am not sure.

We had run out of flour and I went down to the shop for a small bag. It was full of women; they stopped dead when I opened the door. I bought the flour and I held my face for all of them. As I closed the door they began again, all together, as loud as a school-yard.

It is all right when you are angry, and I walked home with nothing but anger for them. But I had left my bag on the counter and I had to go back for it. I was not going to ask one of the men. I was not angry by the time I had walked the road twice: I was afraid. There were more women there and just outside the shop, so they could watch me coming up the road from the bridge. There was Mrs. Williams and her sister from Llan, Mrs. Davies, Pontyfelin, and Mrs. Ifor Bowen, Mrs. Davies, Derw, Miss Jones the Post, the Powells from Garth; there was half the valley and all the village. The women who were not by the shop were at their windows, behind the lace curtains. One or two ran across the street as I went into the shop. It was the silence again, but I was not going to have that, not now that I was prepared. I talked to each woman there, and made her reply; and when I had picked up my bag and went out of the shop I talked to every woman outside too, and made *her* reply. Once I had started it was not hard. They were afraid. I saw they did not dare, and I was very glad.

It had been hard to walk up the hill and although I was

roused now it was harder still to turn my back on them and walk slowly down again.

When I got round past the bridge I sat on the milestone I was trembling so, and when I reached home I went to cry in the barn. I did not care for any one of them, but all together like that, with their hard faces and evil tongues, they daunted me. I did not think I could ever face them again, in case my courage failed.

When I was milking two of them came to see Nain. I do not know what they said, but she was crying too when I came back with the milk.

At that time I kept away from him. I do not know why, unless that it was because I was miserable and I did not want to make him unhappy. He saw, of course.

The house had turned to a sad place. Emyr was still strange, more so indeed, and he kept after me. I had to keep him at his distance, and Nain hated me for it, much more now, poor Nain. The only ones who were not sad were Gerallt and Taid, and of course Llew—he was delighted, and he was spying and running to the village every day. I wondered how Taid could stay so cheerful with sadness all around him. Everybody was pretending to be all right, and he never knew the difference; we must have been good play-actors.

It was then that Mr. Pugh called Emyr in and told him about his idea for putting money into the farm and about leaving Gerallt his heir. Poor Emyr; he was almost torn in two about it. He did so want the money, but he thought that taking it would be giving Mr. Pugh the right to anything he wanted. No, he did not really think that; there was a good side to him that could not think in that base way, but he felt it with the rest of him, and when he took it I am certain—

almost certain—that he felt that that was the bargain. I do not think that he said it to himself, and he would have said it was not true, but I am sure the idea was somewhere in him.

As for Mr. Pugh, it was pure goodness, which Taid understood, even if Emyr could not, altogether. If I could have, I would have loved him even more for it: I did, I believe.

So Emyr came out in two minds. Taid thought he must be mad, and he could not tell Taid why he wanted not to take it: he did bring upsome reasons, and they were so mean I was ashamed for him—it would give Mr. Pugh the right to look in the books and to count the sheep, things like that, and I was the more ashamed for him because they were something worth for him although they were not the main reason.

The more he thought of the money the more he wanted it, and Taid pressed him, so it was agreed.

Nain was so pleased for Gerallt, but her sorrow laid over her happiness. She thought that *that* money was from God; and she went on hating us, both of us, and she did not like the other money, the same way that Emyr did not, although she saw what great use it would be and how it must be taken.

But it all seemed not to matter, to everybody but Taid. At any other time it would have been such a great thing, a time we would have counted everything from, like a fire or a flood, only happy. Now it was just something that had happened, and the house stayed wretched. It is saying a great deal, because to people like us even a little money is very important: you do not forget being hungry, and you fight it off like you would fight fire, beyond reason sometimes.

Mr. Pugh was disappointed, naturally. I was so sorry. I wished I could have made it up to him, but what could I do? I tried to be as cheerful as I could (indeed, I was very glad for

Taid and Gerallt) but I could not pretend with him, not for a moment.

Yes; a wretched house you could call it: but the daily work was to be done, the cooking, cleaning, milking, poultry. Cows and horses must not wait for anything; if there is a death even and you have no neighbors you must go out half an hour after and milk the cows. We had no near neighbor in Cwm Priddlyd, and I did that when my mother died. The pig and the hens, they had to be fed; all the things in the house had to come in their right time and turn.

I began to think it might settle, somehow. I could not see how, when I stopped to think; but when I was working it did not feel quite the same. I worked a great deal. There are always extra things to find that want doing in a house: it was strong work I wanted, not sewing or darning, where I would have to sit and be quiet.

There were some good women in the village, and some more in the farms—but it was a silly, idle kind of half-hope I had. They were hard and wicked for me, even Mrs. Rhys, the kindest there. I went once more, and it was the same: there were fewer of them when I arrived, but more to watch me go. Mair Evans, with the Parrys just behind her, asked me how Mr. Pugh was. She was nothing at all, a drabbling slut, but I could not answer her directly: it was the hardest thing I have ever done to stare her down and tell her that he was much better. I had not got enough anger for it and if she had been a stronger woman I could not have held up. As I went down the hill they laughed. On the road a lorry with men came down from the quarry and they shouted things after me.

The tradesmen who delivered things—we had almost everything delivered—looked at me. Only David Edwards was the same: he was a good man, and he tried to say something about taking no notice once. The postman was the worst, with his snigger, and he was insolent to Mr. Pugh.

When I thought about it, it was Emyr who worried me the worst. He was still so strange, like a man I had never known before: he knew something about what was being said, but how much I did not know, nor what he believed. I did not recognize him again until one afternoon when he had a letter; it was something about money, I thought, because he looked mean—I knew him then. I put the kindling for to-morrow's fire and I saw the envelope in Pritchard Ellis' handwriting, but I did not think to put them together until I had gone upstairs. Emyr was late that night, with the heifer. When he came in, shading the lamp with his hand, I saw his face was red and queer. He did not answer when I asked him about the calf, not naturally, but when he had turned to the window he said he had had to cut it. When he spoke I knew how he was.

He was at the door before me and the light was gone. Oh, there was nothing I could do, nothing, nothing.

This was the worst.

It was Pritchard Ellis who had set him to force me and had worked on him with texts. Emyr. He had tried to bring me gently, and then the devil had got into him again.

He nearly killed me, I think.

But then I could not pity him. I could not think. I was filthy and spoiled. I hated, hated my own body and I hated him. I did not fear him any more—now he had done his beastliness a child could have cut his throat.

But he was not sorry now. He was afraid of me, but not sorry. He could do what he liked and it was right. That was never Emyr alone. I would never be able to master him again: now he had a support besides himself I would never be able to do it.

I wonder now where I got the strength for such hatred. It was because he had spoiled me for *him*. That was the end: I was quite spoiled for him. I had such anger that I could not think, hardly speak. It cowed Emyr. He went under when he had not got the power of his devil.

I could never face *him* again, not look at his good, kind, loving face any more, filthy and abused.

I would not have Emyr in the house, nowhere near me, while my strong evil hatred lasted. He was shaken and cowed. He was frightened, too, when he saw me in the light.

About dinner-time he came out of his room. When he looked in my face the evil went. He was terribly pale, but he smiled somehow to see me.

He knew. He was going out, but he would come back. I took him to the door and watched him till he turned by the barn. He was the dearest man in the world, for me.

The rest. There is not much else. Emyr and Taid had sent for the doctor—I don't remember what he said—I must go to bed. Indeed I could hardly stand any more.

It was a quiet hour while I thought; but my mind was shaken then and my thoughts were poor things, except for him: except when I thought of him they were all run together, not clear. Then Nain came with the physic. She was crying—for me too, I think. She meant to do right: though she would not have seen it that way if we had been more friends.

I was nearly sure what she had done, and I looked at her.

She was crying and she put out her hand. I was sure at the first sip and I drank it off.

I hoped he had not gone too far, because he was still so weak; and that he would not grieve too hard. I cried for him, because he was my only love.

He could not do anything. There was nothing for him to do. I did so hope he would not take the pain too hard.

When it began I told Nain to put the bottle, the foxbottle, in my hand. She was too frightened. I said it hard with all my will, and she did. I dropped it down the side of the bed. That was not to make a great trouble: so that Taid would not know.

It was on me then, and to the end. But he was in my heart and I held to him; so I bore it to the end.

Pugh

hat was it that I had done to them? I could not understand. At times I was almost sure that it was nothing to do with me, but some trouble among themselves. That was certainly there, quite certainly; but was there no more? I could not tell.

It appeared to me sometimes that I must be deceiving myself, and that it was my disordered way of thinking, imagining what did not exist, and my reason for thinking myself mistaken was that the cloud I felt over Gelli now seemed to spread throughout the valley. That could hardly be, I said, and if I was wrong about the second I was wrong about the first: when one is getting better from an illness one's mind still retains the unhealthy melancholy taint. But was I wrong about the second? I was not imagining the surly, withdrawn looks that greeted me in the village, surely? Not imagining them all the time?

I had nothing concrete to go on, no downright rudeness. It was just a strong and general feeling of unfriendliness. Before, it had taken me a quarter of an hour to buy a stamp at the post office, with the necessary talk and interchange; I had thought it a bore sometimes, but now I had my stamp directly. I missed it: I was worried and disorientated.

I was walking about a good deal now, not far, but out every day. On one walk I passed by the small farm just by the village. They had come to see me while I was ill so I did not like to pass the door. I knocked and the woman came to the door: the closed, hard expression on her face drove away my smile. She stood in the door and said that her husband was not at home.

I owe this to Ellis and his good offices, I said as I walked away. I told myself that I should wear it out, or if I did not it could not matter very much: my life had been enclosed and it could be again. If the good opinion of a few odd acquaintances among the farming people was so easily lost it was not of great value. It was sad, though; and I felt it more than I would own at that time.

On my way I met the old woman who had come to do the housework at Hafod: she was an odd figure, with a battered hat perched on her head and a great faggot of brushwood on her back. Without meaning it I had offended her in the past, and although she appeared to bear no malice I intended just to bid her good day and pass by. But she put down her faggot with a grunt and stopped me. "Is sweating, Mr. Pugh," she said, wiping her dirty old face.

"You have a heavy load, Mrs. Bowen," I replied, or something like that. She sat on the bundle and launched into an account of a sack of potatoes that she, or someone else, had carried from one place to another, a great distance, many years ago. I lost the thread very soon. I could never tell whether The damned Thing referred to the sack, her late husband, or some unidentified person in the tale: anyhow, she seemed to have left the original story for that of a parcel from Swansea that was lost in a bus. It was despairing, nervous work listening to her, but I did try to concentrate this time, because I could feel a desire on her part to be friendly—it came through the confusion somehow.

She stopped eventually, from hoarseness, and we said good-by. She pressed my elbow as we parted, and said, "The damned thing, eh?" with an affectionate nod. I wondered what it was as I walked up the hill; there had been references to people in the valley and at Gelli in the later part of her speech. But there was no knowing.

I walked into the kitchen, and Nain was sitting there. It was rare to see any of them sitting and I was going to make some facetious remark when I saw to my horror that she was crying. There was something infinitely pathetic in her frailty, and the brave way she held up her head, disguising it. She wore spectacles; they were always perched on her nose, balancing: the tears gleamed behind them. I feigned not to notice, muttered something, and went quickly to my room.

It was in the course of these days that I noticed a new change in the relations between Nain and Bronwen. I was watching, trying to fathom the cause of all this. They did not quarrel now: it was not exactly quarreling before, but there had been sharp words. Now they spoke rarely, from a distance: it might have been indifference, but it was not, and it was not good-will.

Dear Lord, it was sad, sad: in that odd little room I sat on the edge of the bed with my head in my hands, trying to think clearly. How can you think when you have no clear line to follow? Your head is full of confused dark conjectures; ideas start wildly and end in no conclusion. For me, I found that the habit of logical thought abdicated with hardly a struggle and gave place to melancholy, vague apprehension and worry.

Skinner came up to see me. He had been away for the winter and had come back for a few days before going on to Sweden. He had only just heard that I had been ill. We were very stiff at first and found it difficult to resume our conversation at anything like the pitch it had reached before that unfortunate evening with the Lost Tribes. It must have cost Skinner a lot to come up: he was shy, proud and offended—I honored him for it and doubted whether I should have done as much in his place. I felt very much that I should like to talk pleasantly to him, but it seemed that he could not settle or be easy. We could find nothing to say after the stock of civil inquiries had run out. I worked hard to flog the conversation along, and it was hard work, because I was feeling dull and heavy. The pauses grew more frequent and the topics I dragged up became more and more forced and artificial. I wished he would go away; he had already stayed much longer than was usual for such a visit. But he would not go, and in the end I found out why. After beating about the bush for a good half hour he made a closely qualified statement about the danger and impertinence of meddling. Then, opening and closing his hands as he spoke, and speaking in a hard, formal voice, he said, "I am perfectly well prepared to be told to mind my own business and to be shown the door. I have no wish to interfere with your concerns, Pugh, but they are funny people here and I want to say that you ought to look out for yourself." With that he got up and went straight out of the house.

I was amazed, literally amazed: I did not even have the presence of mind to ask him what he meant (not that he would have said) or even to wish him good-by. I stood gaping at the closed door like a fool.

"What the devil is the good of saying a thing like that if you are not going to amplify it?" I said, sitting down again.

He must have thought that I knew what he was talking about, otherwise what he said had no sense. Perhaps it did have no sense. Perhaps by now he had gone off his head thoroughly; he said he had taken to spiritualism, and that the congress he was going to attend in Sweden was a gathering of spiritualists. He had behaved oddly all the time, and his last remarks had been delivered in a high state of nervous tension—unbalanced, surely?

If it had not been for the behavior of the villagers I should have let it slip from my mind in five minutes as one of Skinner's eccentricities (his house was wired and double-wired against burglars, and the garden was an ironmonger's shop full of patent alarms).

The circumstances being what they were I thought about it for a long time. In the end I thought that I had reached the truth of it: the unfriendliness was the result of Ellis' enmity; for a man in his position nothing could have been easier than to point me out as a scoffer, an unbeliever— anything that required no proof but his opinion. That was one matter: Skinner's warning was another. Someone had talked about this legacy; they might possibly have done that, though they would never have mentioned the investment. The story had run about and had reached Skinner, probably distorted, and he, with his morbid preoccupation with crime and his fanatical attitude toward the Welsh, had instantly concluded that I was in danger of being murdered for my money. Such things have happened, especially in families, and he had probably heard of such a case. It was very decent indeed in him to come up as he had, but what a curious lack of proportion to suppose such a thing in these circumstances. I wondered whether he had ever met Taid or Emyr. It was a satisfactory conclusion.

Both Taid and Emyr came into the yard just then; I heard the ring of their boots and went out to ask them to help me to bring my gramophone down. I had long had it in mind and I had put it off so long only because the machine had a delicate sound-box and horn, and I did not want anyone else to break them: if they were to be broken it would be much better if I did it. I had been longing for music these last days, and now I hoped that it would change my mood for me. I also wanted to see what their reactions would be: there was the national reputation for music, and from what I had learned myself at first hand it was justified. The only time I had been in the dreadful chapel in the village was for an eisteddfod, and I had been deeply impressed by the beauty of the singing in the body of the hall—it was an informal eisteddfod and the audience sang hymns from time to time. I remember, also, the striking contrast between the raw ugliness of that place and the beauty of the voices. It was strange, that partial vision.

We brought the things down, and after supper I proposed

a concert. I had chosen my records carefully; I intended to start with the Kleine Nachtmusik, to go on to the oboe quartet and perhaps to finish with the fifth Brandenburg. They were all things with an instant appeal; or so I had supposed.

They listened politely. The old lady took off her spectacles with a droll, unconscious air of correctness. But I had not turned the first record before I realized that it was no use: they did not hear the music at all, and it was only good manners that kept them in their attentive attitudes. Poor Bronwen: she was far away in some unhappy thoughts of her own. I could not divine them, but it fairly tore my heart to see her, and her sudden attention and interested smile when the record came to an end. I tried a little longer, then gave up and played what few choral pieces I had: that was different, and before the end I had the pleasure of seeing the old man perfectly entranced at a choir singing the Hallelujah Chorus. It may have reached Bronwen, but I do not think it did; she was not far from tears, and when it was finished she went quickly from the room.

It was strange that it should have been like that; but there it was; the fact was obvious and I had to accept it.

That night, with the gramophone in my room, I played over the records that I hoped would purge my sadness. If you put your finger-nail in the sound-track of a revolving record it will play just loud enough for you to hear, with your head bent to your hand. It must be known music, so that memory will supply the phrases that do not come through, or come distorted.

I went on hour after hour. I was far down in the solemn heart-break of the Bach double concerto when I heard a noise in the house. It was a scuffling sound and a thud. I thought I heard a stifled cry: then silence. I was transfixed, squatting there by the machine, listening above the faint whirr of the engine. It turned and turned, ran down slower and slower, and stopped with a little grinding sound. It is easy to start explaining away a noise in the dark. After you have been explaining it for some time you begin to doubt its reality in the first place and it grows insubstantial.

But then in the utter stillness I heard a sobbing, sobbing stifled and kept down, but hopeless, hopeless sobbing that would never stop.

Gray and silent, that is sadness. This was tearing, bitter, so shockingly painful it filled the house; far, far beyond sadness.

All night in that damned chair, with the unfeeling light of the moon: wild, mad schemes tearing through my head in a nightmare, and somewhere in the house that hopeless sobbing, just audible, irregular, killing with pain.

One moment I was on my feet, a Samson and a Hercules, then back in my chair, my rack, whining What can I do, what can I do. What did I do that night long, the only time in my life when I could have been some use? The night long with my love breaking in agony? Nothing. Sat there biting my nails, and sniveled.

I slept some time after the dawn had come in. There are some men who sleep before they are to be hanged. They have to be shaken awake and told to get ready.

Nain brought in my breakfast. I could not talk to her; there were her manners and her deference: an impenetrable wall. I did not come out of my room until nearly twelve. I had heard them in the kitchen. As I opened my door Emyr came in by the outside door: I could not see his face—the sun was behind him—but he was bowed like an old man. I heard Bronwen's voice, low and hard, say, "Out," the word they use to dogs in Welsh; he hesitated, and went, stumbling.

She was standing with her hands on the table. It was another woman there: her face was gray—gray, no color even in her lips, and her enormous eyes were ringed dark. The old people were huddled over by the fire and the child with them. They were frightened. I was still in the bit of passage and as I looked at her I knew what he had done.

When she saw me she smiled, and a human look came into her face.

I stuttered out something about going for a walk, not being hungry. She nodded; there was all of her there. I was to follow her. In the little pantry she cut bread, food wrapped in a paper, and at the door she put her hand on my arm and said, "It will be all right."

I was at the top of Cwm Erchyll, in the dark haunted valley. At one time I must have been deep in the mud of the bog, for it was black and caking on my jacket. Up there there were no clouds, the huge sky and calm: I walked over to where Carnedd and Y Brenin point up, black triangles. They are higher than me; and below was the lake—an easy death down there, the rocks so jagged and the clear air below. But I was not an ineffectual man any more. I had strength too. There were two ravens below me, wheeling in the emptiness, but I had strength now and for me it was clear, plain, no madness or ranting.

The mountains and soft grass, I crossed the mountains

and the soft grass. The lake, I passed that, and the dam. The path now: I was stumbling, lurching with tiredness: stupid with exhaustion I fell—blood somewhere—that quenches your towering fire, and there are hours to go.

It is hard for a man to outrun his body, and train it over twenty miles of mountain, sick at that.

I was talking: you do when you are so beat. Here is the corner; see the good bank of fern. You can kneel down in that and then on all fours you can retch your heart out; you will go better without it. Come on my hero, you have better to do than that, with the long shale ahead. The counties of England; Monmouth and Wales: Ulster, Munster, Leinster and Connaught; and the States of America.

Then doggerel, any sort, in hope of a rhythm for my feet. Never no never no never again: never no never no never again. Never no never no never again.

The ruined sheep-pen and the river. You fall: it is shallow, is another fall important?

They have lit the lamps and from this distance (it is a mile and a half exactly on the Ordnance Survey) there is the usual effect of dancing lights. That comes with fatigue: it can be controlled with resolution. That is the mark, is it not? The effectual man is resolute.

An hour more up there staring over to Carnedd and you would have lain out the night on the mountain.

This is the cart track and level: the rhythm of movement is so important; it will get you there, you know. Never no never no never again never no never no never again.

Yes. The dogs. The door is in front.

———

In the kitchen there was a ghastly pretense of normality. She was in bed: Emyr had brought the doctor. He had said she must go to bed. It was the nerves.

Yes, I said, I had fallen in the water. It was of no consequence. I was going to change. Yes, it was late.

It is hard for a man to outrun his body. It will lie there and not train after him any more then, in the end. I was unconscious across my bed because I had sat for five minutes to gather that famous strength I had found up there, and my resolution.

So I was asleep and in the next day they woke me and the people who woke me were the people who had come hurrying to see her dead.